I0785025

Darryl R. Breland

Starlie's Legacy

From

Tragedy to Triumph

Inspirational Stories Based on True Events

By

Darryl R. Breland

Cover by Anna E. Breland

Darryl R. Breland

Cover art and design by Anna E. Breland

Paperback ISBN: 979-8-9866700-0-3

THIRD EDITION

Starlie's Legacy is Dedicated to the memory of my mother,

Starlie

1935 – 1995

Darryl R. Breland

About the Author:

DARRYL R. BRELAND is a lifelong Mississippian who began writing as a hobby in 2014 with the publication of a two-part series, UnLucky Double, a science fiction. Starlie's Tragedy to Triumph is his third book. His latest works include a history book. His next project will be a series of children's books, The Adventures of Kalamazoo, beginning with Me and You and Kalamazoo.

Learn more about Darryl on Facebook at @BrelandBooks or his website at www.Breland.biz, and his books can be found on Amazon, Barnes and Noble, Smashwords, and other venues.

Other books by Darryl Breland

UnLucky Double Part One

The adventures of Lucky Luciano's double. Sicilian immigrant Giovani Cado rises in the ranks of the New Orleans mafia's bootlegging operation which leads to al Capone recognizing his uncanny resemblance to the infamous Charlie "Lucky" Luciano.

UnLucky Double Part Two

The saga of Lucky's double continues. While on the run from the mob, Cado and his wife is caught by the Nazis in German-occupied France.

History of the Breland Family, from Prussia to Purvis

Written for Darryl Breland's grandchildren, this book chronicles his family history from 1500 to 2022. Available in full color with a hard cover or as a b&w paperback.

Coming Soon: The Adventures of Kalamazoo (A series of children's books)

For ordering information visit: www.Breland.biz and select "My Books"

Darryl R. Breland

Preface

The stories that you are about to read are inspired by actual events. At times, names and places have been changed to protect those desirous of privacy and some stories have been embellished and fictional characters have been added for entertainment value.

Please let me know if you enjoyed reading this book, or how I could have made it better by sending a message through my Facebook page

https://www.facebook.com/BrelandBooks/

Darryl R. Breland

Book reviews beget more sales.

Please support me by

being kind and reviewing this book.

Thank you!

Darryl Breland

Table of Contents

Introduction

Starlie was an extraordinary person. If you had met her, you would have seen a most humble person. One lacking self-confidence, especially in a crowd. This is ironic because she was the strongest and bravest woman to everyone who knew her.

She had few clothes, and they were made of cheap fabric, typically polyester, devoid of fashion. Those who saw her regularly would notice she wore the same clothes often, for many years. But her clothes were always clean, and she made sure her children and husband had what they needed before she considered her own needs. That explains why she dressed the way she did. There wasn't enough money left over for her to spend on herself, but she never complained. Not once.

Starlie missed the opportunity to receive a formal education. But don't make the mistake of thinking she wasn't smart, or informed. She loved to read and was self-taught. She sometimes struggled to find the proper words, and her grammar was poor, but when she spoke, everyone who knew her, respected her words. She was the wisest woman I've ever known.

If anyone deserved a better life, it was her. Many of us owe so much to her, including our very lives. Despite her hardships, she wasn't a bitter person, just the opposite. She was most unselfish and kind. Much of her life was tragic, but she never felt sorry for herself or allowed anyone else to treat her as a victim.

When there was an important decision to be made, she listened to others first, but when expressed her opinion, her decision was final, and everyone agreed. We all knew that she was wiser and smarter than us – including her husband and parents. She was the family matriarch and the glue which held us together.

Some of the stories in this book may seem unrelated to her, but none of these stories would have been possible if it hadn't been for the most courageous actions taken by Starlie when she was a mere child. This is her story and legacy.

Chapter 1: Ernest

Ilda Waters hated conflict, but when her husband, the doctor, was away, she became the medical clinic's final authority, the one to turn to in sensitive matters. Alice, the clinic's human resources manager, explained the situation. "A patient reported that Ernest groped her and then brandished a knife in a threatening manner and whispered that he would kill everyone here if she reported him."

Ilda placed her elbows on the desk and paused to ponder the situation before replying, "She obviously didn't take the threat seriously, or she wouldn't have reported him."

This wasn't the first time there had been complaints about the maintenance manager. Although Ernest was a handsome man with a charming smile, he was described by some as dark and creepy. One minute he could win you over, and make you believe anything, but the next moment, with nothing more than a glare, he could also strike fear in you. He was a big man, towering over most, and well fit. Although he was married, he never hesitated to make a pass at a female whom he considered attractive, or submissive, be it a patient, or clinic nurse.

Alice spoke without hesitation, for she had seen both sides of Ernest, "She didn't."

With a quizzical expression asked, "Who did then?"

"The girl's mother." Knowing further explanation was required, Alice continued, "The patient is only thirteen… she was by herself in the room waiting for the nurse when he walked in and pretended to be the doctor. Vanessa walked in and asked him what he was doing in there, and that's when Ernest turned his back to Vanessa, faced the girl, and whispered in her ear before telling Vanessa that he was there to prepare the room for installing an air conditioner."

Although wintertime, the clinic had committed to investing in the fairly new technology which, considering Houston's blistering summers, would come as a welcome relief.

"How is the girl?" Ilda asked.

"The girl didn't tell Vanessa what Ernest said or did, and would not say what was wrong, but she seemed nervous and scared. Vanessa wanted to report this to me right away, but Ernest shadowed her, letting her know she was being watched."

There was a pause. Both women were waiting for the other to speak next when Alice continued. "Then, I received a call from the girl's mother, Mrs. Torres, who explained."

"The girl took the threat seriously enough to warn us," Ilda replied.

"Yes, so I called Vanessa into my room to verify her side of the story, and I noticed Ernest watching us as she entered and exited my office."

"Oh my God, he is so scary. I so wish Dr. Waters were here now."

"I have more bad news. Vanessa turned in her resignation and didn't even finish her shift."

Ilda leaned back in her chair. Now she was no longer scared, but angry. Vanessa was a reliable nurse, and threatening patients could put the clinic that she and her husband had worked hard to establish, out of business. "I suppose that I need to tend to this right away before we lose any more employees or patients," Ilda said as she stood and moved from behind her desk. "But I need to talk to Mrs. Torres first."

Ilda thanked Alice for her bravery, and as she opened the door for her to exit the office, both women noticed Ernest at the end of the hall, toolbox in hand. He wanted them to know he was aware of Vanessa's betrayal.

Ilda grabbed Alice by the arm, stopping her from walking away, and whispered, "Have every man who works for us today meet in our conference room in one hour. Don't tell them what's going on and to keep quiet about this emergency meeting."

Most Texas doctors were men in the 1940s, and nearly all nurses were women. There were two doctors on duty that day, and both promptly went to Ilda to discover the meaning of the secret emergency meeting. Once briefed, the doctors agreed to the plan, which was to have the nurses and female administrative staff continue working as usual and have the male employees escort Ernest off the property. He was, after all, a big man with broad shoulders and barrel-chested, not to mention likely armed with a knife.

The other men working in the office included an accountant, a balding middle- aged man who was meek and mild-mannered, but two of the custodians were young black men who appeared to be in top physical condition. One was tall and scrappy, and the other was as big as Ernest.

Ernest had facial features that disagreed with his chosen occupation. He looked more like a salesman, a politician, or an actor with a full head of dark hair. When he wasn't menacing, he could be charming. Those who didn't know him described him as a handsome and trusting man. People who knew him well described him as frightful and evil. His eyes were bright blue and piercing. His eyes always betrayed his smile, which some said that it was if he was smiling because he knew that he had evil plans for you. He must have appeared even more menacing to Ilda and her comrades at that moment. He was standing tall and had a hammer in his right hand.

The quickly organized posse couldn't find him easily at first. Ernest appeared aware of our plan and was evading capture. When the staff was questioned if they had seen him or knew of his whereabouts, a couple mentioned that they had seen him working on the office windows. "He said he was preparing them for installing air conditioners," one employee said.

With a doctor on each side of her and Alice at a safe distance behind them, Ilda said to Ernest, "Mr. Hollingsworth, I need a word with you. Would you please come to my office?"

Despite his blue pupils, Ernest's eyes appeared very dark at that moment. He wasn't smiling when he replied, "No ma'am. I don't care to." The following silence was deafening for the next several seconds. All eyes were on the hammer that Ernest gripped tightly.

"What are you doing with that hammer?" Ilda asked.

A brief smile appeared on his lips, as he realized that he was more intimidating than ever with the potentially deadly object firmly in his grasp. He tossed it into his open toolbox, creating a collective sigh of relief, then he said, "Doing my job."

To avoid prolonging this potentially violent situation, Ilda got to the point. "This is a very unpleasant thing for me to do, but I must ask you to leave this place immediately. Your employment is terminated, and you are no longer welcome here."

Ernest presented his infamous smile and for the first time began to move his body, swaying, then twisting and turning, but his feet weren't moving. After an excruciating minute of silence, he reached into the toolbox and once again had the hammer in his hand. Ilda's heart pounded with fear. She could feel the doctors pulling her gently so that their shoulders were in front of her. The custodians stepped forward and gave Ernest menacing expressions.

Ernest closed the toolbox and latched it with his free hand. Looking straight into Ilda's eyes, he said, "You felt it necessary to bring protection?" Then he barked an insincere short laugh. "Those weaklings can't do you no good. I could bash their skulls in so fast."

The scrappy custodian had to be held back by one of the doctors and the other doctor said in the firmest tone his gentle voice could muster, "All right that's enough tough guy!" and then turned to Ilda and said, "You've notified him, and he is being belligerent, so go call the police. We will stay with him until they get here."

"Not necessary. I ain't working anywhere that I'm not wanted. I'll put these tools away and be on my way."

Ilda replied, "No need; we will put those where they belong. You can just leave them right here."

Ernest ignored Ilda and picked up the toolbox with his left hand, still sporting the hammer in his right hand; holding it as if he were ready to strike something or someone with it at any moment and began making his way to the door.

The doctors quickly moved to the side of the room, giving plenty of clearance between Ernest and the door. Ilda exited the room ahead of Ernest. The doctors were relieved when Ernest walked past them without incident, through the doorway, and down the hall. The waiting area was empty; Alice had seen to that. The frightened staff, protected somewhat by a glass enclosure, pretended not to notice Ernest walking out the front door with the clinic's toolbox and hammer.

Within minutes of his departure, the staff hand an impromptu meeting consisting of tears, hugs, and words of encouragement. This was not the first time Ernest had given various staff members a reason to celebrate his leaving. Valuables began to disappear shortly after his employment began and he had made inappropriate remarks to virtually every female employee.

The celebration was short-lived as someone noticed smoke flowing rapidly in from underneath the front door and the floor furnace vents. The collective emotions quickly changed to panic. One of the cooler heads hurried to open the front door, but it was nailed shut and had a metal bar chained across to make doubly sure no one escaped through the door. Someone screamed, "The door is locked from the outside! Try the windows!"

The employees scampered, a couple of them pulled back window curtains almost in synchronicity to reveal that they had been boarded up! It must have occurred to Ilda at that moment what Ernest was really doing when he said he was preparing the windows.

The following day, investigators determined that someone had chained all the exterior doors from the outside and set the building ablaze, and boarded most of the windows.

The survivors escaped when the custodians used their strength and chairs to break the windows and the boards that had been erected. Unfortunately, Ilda Waters did not survive, and even more, unfortunately, for reasons unknown, no one was ever charged with the crime – but Ilda's husband, Dr. Waters thought he knew the culprit.

Chapter 2: Starlie

Starlie was born in Kingsville, Texas, on October 2, 1935. Anna Mae named her beautiful baby girl Starlie because "when I look at her, I feel as though I am in heaven, and she is the brightest star."

I knew Anna Mae as Grandma. Many years later, Grandma worked for the Carnation Ice Cream factory in Houston. As an employee, she was able to take home ice cream sandwich rejects and tubs of ice cream. I loved visiting Grandma. And she loved our visits and it showed. She would always have the latest comic books for us when we arrived. Spiderman was my favorite, and she knew it.

What a treat it was when my grandmother took me on a tour of an ice cream factory! The free ice cream and cookies at Carnation Foods were better than a trip to Astro-World. Speaking of Astro-World, every trip to visit Grandma included a trip to Astro-World, a tour of the Astrodome, the Houston Zoo, and the Science Museum.

Sometimes we were treated to a tour of the Humble Building, which was the tallest building in Houston in the 1960s, a mind-boggling forty-four stories tall. I recently visited Houston and a forty-four-story is hard to find among the forest of taller skyscrapers.

Anna Mae's second husband, Joe, was the only grandfather on my mother's side of the family that I ever knew – thankfully. Anna Mae and Joe had a pool table in their quaint home. The whole family, including small children such as me, were given the opportunity to play. To keep playing, you had to win, and everyone in my family including Anna Mae, and especially Grandpa Joe could shoot the lights out in pool. The whole family would play for hours and hours, day after day. When we weren't playing pool, we enjoyed the front porch swing.

Due to a stroke, Grandpa Joe was confined to a wheelchair. Anna Mae loved him, cared for him, and pampered him to the day he died. How could anyone be cruel to sweet Anna Mae? The same could be said about my mother, Starlie, and any of her four sisters. Only a truly evil person could be cruel to such kind people. Unfortunately, Anna Mae's first husband and the father to her five daughters was such a man – cruel and evil.

Most of what I know about Ernest I read in my Aunt Christine's autobiography, "Wading Through Deep Waters," and oral conversations with my mother, Starlie, and my father, Charles Breland.

I may never understand why Anna Mae married Ernest Hollingsworth in the first place, but she did. She even divorced him and remarried him. Maybe she had what would later be known as Stockholm Syndrome. No one can say for certain, but there are theories.

The more that I learned about Ernest, the more apparent it became that Anna Mae was a virtual slave to Ernest. She was totally controlled by her fear of him. Even in modern times, there are women who are controlled as sex slaves. Apparently, modern-day slave masters force their slaves to become addicted to drugs to control them, but fear is the greatest motivator of all because I don't think Anna Mae ever used drugs. There is no doubt that Anna Mae was extremely afraid of Ernest.

On the day that Starlie was born, Ernest was furious that Anna Mae had not given him a son. Instead of sharing the joys of becoming a parent for the first time, Ernest verbally abused Anna Mae daily until she had recovered enough from childbirth to handle a beating, according to his standards. He beat her badly many times and told her that the beatings would stop when she provided him with a son. When he wasn't beating her, he was virtually raping her. According to most state laws at that time, a man could not be charged for raping his wife, but I am sure that Anna Mae felt as if she was being raped. She was made to feel as if her only purpose in life was to serve Ernest. He owned her. She was his property.

A year or so later, Anna Mae was pregnant again. She prayed

for a boy so the beatings would stop. Two years after Starlie was born, Anna Mae gave birth to another baby girl named Earline. The beatings and verbal abuse continued. Anna Mae was abused by Ernest in every way a person can be abused. She was humiliated in front of Ernest's poker buddies. Although it was never said, I was given the impression that Ernest forced Anna Mae to be with his poker buddies from time to time, possibly as the result of losing a wager in which he put her up in lieu of cash.

Ernest would often announce that they were moving to another city, usually in Texas, but they would occasionally live in Mobile, Alabama, or Pensacola, Florida. Pensacola was Ernest's hometown, and Mobile was Anna Mae's hometown, but Anna Mae suspected that Ernest was fleeing to escape justice for a crime that he had committed. Anna Mae and Ernest first met in Mobile and eventually were married. Anna Mae, like her mother and father, was a kind soul and devout Christian.

Ernest was the opposite and being married to him must have been a living nightmare for Anna Mae. He was a brutal man and a hard drinker. He would leave his family alone for days or weeks without revealing where he had been or when he would return. Anna Mae learned not to question his whereabouts or how he made a living. Sometimes he would come home with blood on his clothes but had no apparent injuries on his body. Anna Mae would be required to scrub his clothes until there was no sign of blood.

Years before Starlie was born, Anna Mae miscarried, possibly because of a beating imposed upon her by Ernest. He was so enraged by the loss of the baby because he thought it was a boy that he flew into one of his infamous violent rages, but this time, Anna Mae had had enough. She left him and filed for divorce. For a short time, she was free of the monster, but he returned, and by some method beyond my comprehension, convinced her to remarry him. My mother and father both theorized that it was fear that motivated her to remarry him. They learned many years later that Anna Mae was convinced that if she did not do exactly as Ernest demanded, he would kill her and her whole family, including her children and parents.

Anna Mae gave birth to yet another baby girl, Christine, in 1942. World War II was raging, Starlie was seven years old, and Earline was five. Once again, Anna Mae was blamed for not providing Ernest with a son.

The rapes, beatings, and abuse continued. Many years later, my aunt Christine Broadus, wrote in her book, *Wading Through Deep Waters*, about her life growing up as Ernest's daughter:

"When I was about three years old, Daddy got a job in Houston, Texas. All of us, Mother, Daddy, Starlie, Earline, and I moved out there...Not long after that, things happened in our home that would have a terrible effect upon my young life and forever etched in my memories. Being so young at the time, I'm sure the exact details and dates are somewhat confused. But the scenes are still vivid in my mind. I recall Daddy coming home from work when I was five or six years old. I saw him walking down the sidewalk...he was kind of wobbling and staggering."

Anna Mae instructed her children to be "real quiet" to not upset their daddy. The children had been having fun, laughing, and playing, but now the mood had changed. Everyone was tense and nervous.

Fearing the consequences of upsetting him, Anna Mae made every effort to please Ernest, but nothing that she could do would prevent him from becoming more belligerent.

Anna Mae was relieved when one of his drinking buddies arrived because his attention would turn away from abusing his family; or so, she thought. The men sat at the small kitchen table, playing cards, and drinking whiskey. Soon they were drunk. Ernest told the girls to go into the bedroom and not make a sound. They hurriedly obeyed, frightened "like mice." Ernest spoke loudly as he stomped his foot, *"Listen to what happens when*

I stomp my foot." Anna Mae rushed to his side, ready to take instructions. Ernest demonstrated with pride to his drunken companion that he had trained his wife to be obedient and to come running to his service with a stomp of his foot.

I cannot express to you how difficult it was for me to read, and then recount what my Aunt Christine wrote next in her book.

> *"Years later I found out that after we children were in bed, Daddy made Mother do things with his friends that are too embarrassing for me to ever write about. It is my understanding that it happened on many occasions. I do believe that my daddy was controlled by the devil."*

Ernest had complete control over Anna Mae because she feared that he would kill her after making her watch her children being killed. She had good reason to believe that he was capable of such an act.

His drinking buddies often visited to play cards throughout the night. Once, Anna Mae could hear a player laughing and bragging about how much money he had taken from Ernest. After the sun had risen, Ernest suggested to the player they end the card game and go fishing. The buddy agreed and the two left together. Ernest returned with all his money, and the other man was never seen or heard from again.

Years later, my father, Charles, recounted a story about the time Ernest asked him to go fishing. He had not yet married my mother, Starlie. Charles said, "Your mother told me that day to never turn my back on him, especially if there is a knife in his hand. When you sit in that boat, make sure that you are always facing him."

World War II ended in 1945, and Anna Mae gave birth to yet another girl. Ernest was livid once again that he wasn't given a boy. They named their new daughter, Ilda. We don't know whose idea it was to name her after Ilda Waters who died tragically in the arson fire. Surely Anna Mae knew nothing of the possibility of Ernest being complicit in her death. My guess is that she did not, and it was Ernest's idea to name her Ilda as a cruel gesture to Dr. Waters, and possibly to thumb his nose at investigators. He may have been telling the world, "Yes, I did it, but you can't prove it."

Despite not having a formal education and his constant relocation from city to city, Ernest lived well. At one point, he owned his own airplane, then another. He even owned a drug store, Hollingsworth Pharmacy, for a while. His good fortune wasn't shared with his family. His girls had to wear homemade clothes, sometimes made from croaker sacks. A croaker sack is a wool bag. Holes were cut for a head and two arms to slip through. I imagine this wool sack having been modified to serve as a dress would have been terribly uncomfortable and extremely embarrassing for the children to wear. I remember once as a child, complaining about being embarrassed because I had to wear hand-me-downs to school, and my mother told me about her having to wear a croaker sack dress to school, so I should be thankful. I am now.

There were times when my mother and her sisters were so hungry as children, Anna Mae had to stop them from eating raw chicken. Ernest would not allow his wife or children to accept charity from others, not even the local church pastor.

Christine explained in her book the first time he witnessed her father beat her mother:

> *"Mother had started taking us girls to church. Not long after, she began playing piano for them. We were very poor, and everyone knew it. The pastor told Mother that some people in the church wanted to give us some things. He came to the house and brought Mother several nice dresses and a heater. Well, like most other evenings, Daddy came home drunk. First, he wanted to know what the heater was doing there. Mother explained that the pastor had brought it along with some dresses for her. She told Daddy how much she appreciated it.*
>
> *Daddy instantly went into a rage. He took an ax, chopped away at the heater, and destroyed it. He*

then took it to the pastor's home and left it on his front porch. When Daddy came back, he took out his knife and cut Mother's dresses to shreds. Mother was crying and begging him not to do it, but he didn't stop. He then began to slap and beat Mother. I was so frightened. Although I was terribly afraid of Daddy when he was like this, I still loved him."

Christine begged her father, "Please Daddy, don't do this! Please stop! Please don't hit mother anymore!"

She was about six years old at the time. Ernest turned around and "put one hand behind my head and hit me in the face with his fist. I was later told that if he had not put his hand behind my head, he would have broken my neck," Christine explained. Anna Mae was so ashamed of the things that Ernest had done, that "she never went back to that church."

Each time that I've attempted to write or re-write the rest of this story, I am required to take a break so that I can get control of my emotions. I am not ashamed to tell you that I must clear the tears from my eyes, and I have to force myself to sit back down to write, but my mother deserves her story to be told. More importantly, this story needs to be told to countless other women and children who may be in similar circumstances.

Christine described the first time that she became aware that my mother, Starlie was sexually abused by her father:

"Late one night I heard a lot of noise in their room. In just a little while I saw my sister Starlie, who was about twelve years old, come running out of Daddy's bedroom in her panties and bra. Daddy chased after her in his underwear. She ran out the back door, and he followed. She was crying, 'Daddy, please don't! Please, Daddy, stop! Please, Daddy!'

I don't know where Mother was or what happened that night, but I found out later that Daddy had sexually abused Starlie. It had gone on for a long time," Christine writes. "Daddy also beat Starlie. One time he said she had lied to him. She cried, begged, and told him she was telling the truth. But in his drunken rage, he beat her with a belt and then turned around and beat her with the buckle. Mother was wringing her hands and begging Daddy to stop. But it didn't matter to him. He just kept on beating her while we watched and cried."

Starlie wasn't the only one of Ernest's daughters to be abused. Earline suffered too. Once Anna Mae had taken Starlie, Earline, and Christine for a walk in the neighborhood park. Upon returning, they noticed broken dishes and garbage strewn across the front porch and yard. Ernest was in a rage because Anna Mae had left dirty dishes in their kitchen sink before going for a walk. One by one, starting with Anna Mae, then Starlie, then Earline, he dished out severe beatings.

When the fifth daughter, Eunice was born in 1948, Ernest was so furious that Anna Mae had not given him a boy he flew into another violent rage. When Anna Mae returned from the hospital with Eunice, Ernest, in a drunken rage, grabbed his shotgun and threatened to kill Anna Mae.

Seeing that he was a madman, Anna Mae picked up Eunice, hoping Ernest would not shoot her with the baby in her arms. Earline, who was only eleven, ran and put herself in front of Anna Mae and baby Eunice. Eventually, Ernest calmed down and put the gun away. That would not be the last time that Earline took action to save her family.

While that incident was taking place, Starlie ran out of the house and down the street and into the nearest place of business, a corner pub, where she pleaded for someone to help her because her daddy was trying to kill her mother. No one would help. They did not even call the police. What kind of people ignores the pleas of a terrified little girl?

There were many incidents of abuse and terror over the years for Anna Mae and her daughters, and things didn't get better, they continually got worse. Within a short walking distance of their home in Mobile, there was a corner grocer. In those days, the local grocer knew everyone in the neighborhood, including the children.

Children commonly picked up groceries for the family without having to pay on the spot. The grocer would enter the purchase on a log and once each month customers would settle their bill. This store, Howell's Grocery, provided a delivery boy to help customers with getting their purchases home safely. Charles was the delivery boy when Starlie met him. She was fourteen and he was seventeen.

Charles was the second of ten children. His father was a fire-and-brimstone Church of God preacher. In fact, Grandpa Breland, as I knew him, was one of the early founders of the Holiness Church of God in Mississippi. Charles's mother took their religion seriously as well. I was told that she never cut her hair, never wore make-up, and never wore pants. They were, what were and are often referred to as "Holy Rollers."

As a child, I remember that the first thing that children my age had to do upon first arriving at Grandpa and Grandma Breland's home, was to pick peas and beans and shuck corn. We had to do those miserable chores for hours before we were allowed to play.

Grandpa was zealous about religion, but that didn't keep him from having a sense of humor. Grandpa and Grandma Breland had been married for over fifty years when she passed away. Despite being eighty-eight years old, Grandpa was still in good health, preaching the gospel on a regular basis, when he married his second wife. She passed away two years later. Four years after that, Grandpa traveled to Europe and toured Normandy, where his son had fought. He was ninety-four years of age. Upon his return, the family reunited to celebrate Thanksgiving at his home, as had been the tradition for many years. One of his granddaughters, and my cousin, Susan, asked Grandpa Breland, "Grandpa, you are still in such good health, traveling to Europe recently, remarrying just a few years ago...I'm curious, would you ever remarry again?"

Without hesitation, Grandpa Breland answered, "Oh no. That would be totally unfair of me."

"Why?" Susan asked.

"Well, you see, ever since they invented Viagra, I've been wearing women out."

With an embarrassed chuckle, Susan responded, "Why don't you simply stop taking Viagra then?"

Again, without hesitation, he answered, "Then I would start rolling out of bed again!"

There are some who will take offense at such remarks because it somehow demeans women, but it was a man's world in those days, as it was in the proceeding 240,000 years. More than that, the fact that it was said by someone whom I imagined as a prude, made it more humorous.

Charles began courting Starlie, and their romance was a whirlwind. I speculate that my mother was in desperate need of being rescued from her father. Charles, who had a heart as big as Texas, was easy to fall in love with. He offered her protection and a life free from terror and abuse. Who can blame her? Charles was a kind, gentle, and honest person with Christian-family values deeply ingrained. Charles told me that he did not know what Starlie was experiencing with her father before he married her. That knowledge may or may not have made a difference in his decision to marry Starlie. Thankfully, she said yes, and they secretly drove over to Mississippi, chaperoned by Anna Mae, where it was legal to get married at age fourteen with parental consent.

Charles' mother and father were not happy at all to learn the news of their son's clandestine marriage. He had just finished the tenth grade and would never return to school. Charles' mother called Anna Mae the following morning inquiring to learn if Anna Mae knew of his whereabouts. "Charles has not been home all night," Grandma Breland said. Anna Mae put down the phone and tried to think of a way to break the news to Charles' mother. Anna Mae said, "I believe they are on their honeymoon."

Anna Mae likely saw that this marriage was Starlie's best chance of escaping constant mental, physical and sexual abuse, and they both likely knew that a child was the best way to solidify a marriage. Think what you will, but despite my mother being married at age fourteen and giving birth to her first child at age fifteen, neither she nor my father ever applied for or received, any government assistance or welfare in their lifetime. Over the years, our electricity and water were turned off for late payments. We ate a lot of beans and rice. To mix things up, we would have rice and beans. But, despite the hard times, we never once resorted to seeking government assistance. We had too much pride.

Despite their disappointment, Charles' mother and father allowed Starlie and Charles to live with them until they could afford their own place.

Everyone knew there would be big trouble once Ernest discovered that Starlie and Charles had married. He was in Texas working at the time. Upon learning the news, he threatened to kill Charles, Anna Mae, her mother, and father, and basically the entire family for betraying him. Everyone involved was suffering from anxiety because they knew that his threats should not be taken lightly. A few days later, on a Saturday, Ernest returned to Mobile, arriving by train. It was early morning when he approached Anna Mae's family home, the McDuffie's house, and Christine was excited. No matter how wicked of a man he was, Ernest was the only father that she had ever known. She ran as fast as she could to meet him. Ernest picked her up and held her high. She was too young to know what was going on and what was in store for the family.

Ernest asked for Earline. Grandma McDuffie said calmly, to Christine's surprise, "I guess she is still sleeping." She knew that wasn't true. Earline wasn't there. She had gotten up early that morning and taken a city bus to the police station.

Anna Mae's father, known as Grandpa McDuffie, sat in a chair across the room with a shotgun by his side, with one hand on it always. He knew what Ernest could do and was prepared to protect his family.

Anna Mae's mother, Grandma McDuffie, who looked and dressed like an Indian squaw, stood barely five feet tall by his side. I had the pleasure of knowing Grandma McDuffie, for she lived to be 99 years of age, dying when I was about twelve years old.

Possibly discouraged by the shotgun, Ernest informed Anna Mae's parents that he was going to the Dew Drop Inn, a nearby pub, to hang out for a little while. Shortly after Ernest left, a police car arrived, asking for "Mr. Hollingsworth." Anna Mae's mother told the officers that Ernest had left, but they expected him to return. Christine recalls the policemen asking her if she had ever been hurt or abused by her father. Christine answered, "No."

Mobile is an old city, by American standards, and is blessed to have an abundance of beautiful large trees known as Spanish oaks. These trees grow enormous limbs that twist and stretch out far to provide a canopy over many of the streets. Soon thereafter, Ernest was seen walking on the canopy-covered city sidewalk which leads to the McDuffie house. The policemen asked him to identify himself and then told him to get into the police car. He didn't resist. That was the last time that Christine saw her daddy.

Twelve-year-old Earline, fearing that her father fully intended to carry out his threats to kill the whole family, made her way to the police department and told the police everything she knew about her father's abuse of her, her sisters, and her mother. They questioned her for hours over and over to make certain that her story never changed before they made the decision to arrest Ernest. The district attorney arrived and questioned her also, then made the decision to issue an arrest warrant.

Behind bars, Ernest asked if he could see his daughter, Earline. The district attorney granted his request, but accompanied Earline, keeping her beyond her father's reach.

Ernest said, "Come here to daddy, darling. You know you love me, and that I love you. Now, tell the police that what you have said is a lie. You know daddy hasn't done all these things."

Earline said, "Daddy, you know it is true, and I will not change my story."

She was a very brave girl. She never had to face her father again, but she suffered torment for the remainder of her life.

The district attorney told the court at his hearing, that how Ernest had treated his family was the worst that he had ever heard, and "Mr. Hollingsworth deserves the most severe punishment that the court has to offer."

Ernest's sisters were there that day. According to my family, they knew what kind of man he was, but they denied it, claiming that he was a kind and gentle man.

Ernest spent several months in jail awaiting his trial, but despite the threats that he had made to his family and the D.A. warning the court over and over not to do it, he was released on bond. The D.A. instructed Ernest to "not leave Mobile, and definitely do not go near your family."

Upon learning that Ernest was free on bond, the entire

family was frightened. Starlie and Charles had relocated to Houston, Texas, where he worked at a grocery store. They were expecting their first child. Anna Mae was there at the time, helping to care for Starlie.

Christine and her two younger sisters were living with their grandparents, the McDuffie's home, in Mobile. They would see Ernest occasionally drive by the house day and night. The children were not allowed to go outside the house. Then one day, he stopped driving by the house.

Ernest managed to learn the whereabouts of Starlie, Charles, and Anna Mae. He drove to Houston to find them. It was Christmastime. Starlie had given birth barely a month before to a baby boy that they named David. It must have been a terrible shock to Starlie and Anna Mae when Ernest arrived at their door. Charles was at work. At first, Ernest acted as if all was forgiven and that he was so happy to see his newborn grandson. "Finally, I have the boy that I've always wanted," he said.

They knew that it was just a ruse. They were gripped with terror, and justifiably so. The apartment where they lived was small, so everyone was in close quarters. As expected, Ernest began drinking, and soon he was drunk. He then produced a piece of paper that he demanded Starlie sign stating that everything that was told to the police was a lie. Starlie refused, stating that she and Earline had told the truth.

More infuriated than ever, Ernest put a knife to baby David's throat and said, "You either sign that paper or I will kill this little bastard."

Starlie signed the paper so that Ernest would cool down and remove the knife from David's throat. She then offered to make a pallet on the floor for him. "You must be exhausted from the long trip," she said.

Ernest stretched out of the pallet made for him in the middle of the floor, then just before going to sleep pointed to David and said, "The first thing that I'm going to do when I wake up is to kill that bastard."

Starlie and Anna Mae had a monumental decision to make. They believed beyond any doubt that it was just a matter of time before Ernest killed them all. Charles and Anna Mae's parents were likely in danger too. They didn't trust the police or the courts to protect them. He had managed to escape the Alabama court system. Running and hiding wasn't a safe option, after all, he had found them in Houston. They discussed their options for hours until they knew what had to be done.

Anna Mae may have regretted her decision which resulted

in Starlie having to suffer greatly for the rest of her life. Anna Mae convinced Starlie to be the one to pull the trigger because being a minor, Starlie was more likely to spend less time in prison than her.

Charles was left out of the discussion. He and Starlie had not known one another very long, and she likely had not told him the embarrassing details about her father. Had he known, he may have been the one to protect the family. I know I would have.

In any event, my mother unloaded the shotgun on her father as he slept, killing him instantly. Then she immediately called the police and confessed to what she had done. When the police arrived, Starlie, who was barely fifteen at the time, kept asking "Is he dead?" She was shaking and terrified of the prospect he would recover from his gunshot wounds and return to get his revenge. She likely suffered nightmares for years, if not for the entirety of her life.

Houston investigators discovered that Ernest had been freed on bond in a Mobile court. When the Houston authorities contacted the Mobile district attorney, he told them the terrible things that Ernest had done to his family, and said, "he should have been killed a long time ago, I'm just sorry that his little girl had to do it. You should not press charges on her. Let them all go in peace."

The Houston authorities agreed with the D.A. from Mobile and told Starlie that she was free to go. Newspaper headlines across the country featured the story of the little girl who killed her father. Tabloid magazines tried to interview my mother, but she declined. At least one tabloid printed the story with her picture anyway. That picture can be seen on this book's cover. She was embarrassed and ashamed about the entire ordeal. She also felt guilt that plagued her until the day she died. The wounds that fateful night left deep scars on my entire family. I don't just mean those who were living at the time, but even those of us who weren't born until years later were all affected by the events of that night.

The day the news story broke, Starlie got a call from a Texas doctor. She had never heard of Dr. Waters. He called to tell her that had read about her story and that he was willing to fund the entire cost of her defense if she were to ever be indicted for killing her father. The doctor explained he suspected Ernest had set the fire that killed his wife and employees. Thankfully, she never had to accept his offer.

Starlie as a child

Starlie and Charles

Chapter 3: Tragedy

On January 1, 1995, Starlie had settled comfortably on her sofa after eating black-eyed peas and cabbage, as was her tradition. Another of her traditions was to telephone all of those she loved to wish them a Happy New Year.

Ray, her second husband, was reclined in his easy chair, eyes half-closed, trying to pay attention to the football game on the television. At one point he became aware that he hadn't heard Starlie say anything to anyone on the telephone for an extended period. Looking her way, he saw that she was sitting upright but her head was slumped forward. Her eyes were closed. The phone was "off the hook," as we used to say when a landline telephone handset had not been placed on its base after a call had ended. It appeared that she had dropped the phone with a call in progress. Ray called out to her, but she did not respond. He heard a barely discernable voice coming from the telephone handset. He got up and shook her in hopes of waking her, but she did not wake, she fell gently to her left onto the sofa. Ray picked up the telephone and asked, "Who is this?"

Ray's son explained that Starlie had gone suddenly silent in mid-conversation. He had been calling out to her to see if she was all right. Landline phone calls were rarely terminated, or "dropped" due to technical issues, and everyone knew that

Starlie did not have a cell phone. Ray told his son he needed the phone to call for emergency help because Starlie was unconscious.

Starlie and Ray had been married for thirty years. Life was a struggle for most of those years, considering they raised his and her children together. But life had improved in recent years since they became "empty-nesters." They had a spacious home compared to the tiny two-bedroom home that was occupied by as many as seven people at one point in time. This home was nestled among a pecan orchard on a large city lot in Pascagoula, Mississippi. Ray had always wanted a swimming pool, but couldn't afford one when he was supporting children, nor was there room for one in the tiny yard where his previous home was situated. He finally got the swimming pool he always wanted.

Starlie and Ray had plans to travel and see the world; something they could have only dreamed about during the many difficult years of juggling money just to keep the lights on.

The only thing holding them back was Anna Mae. She had suffered from several strokes and debilitating Alzheimer's disease. Anna Mae and her second husband, Joe, relocated to Pascagoula from Houston to be close to Starlie several years ago. Joe passed away shortly thereafter. Anna Mae was confined to a nursing home and Starlie considered herself her mother's caregiver. She and Ray postponed their plans to travel while Anna Mae was alive. Other than an occasional stomach ulcer, Starlie was in good health, and at fifty-nine, she was expected to be around for many more years. She had plenty of time left to enjoy life after her mother passed, we thought.

Pascagoula is situated on the eastern shore of the Mississippi Gulf Coast, just a few miles west of Mobile, Alabama. At the time, I lived in Madison, Mississippi with my wife, Catherine, and my sixteen-month-old son, Bailey. Madison was at least a three-hour drive from Pascagoula in those days because self-flying cars had yet to be invented. We arrived at Pascagoula's Singing River Hospital much less than three hours after receiving the call that my mother was in the intensive care unit. Ray, my sister, Wanda, and my brother, David, were there before us. We all waited for hours before a doctor came to give us a report.

Starlie's prognosis was not good. She was in a deep coma, but the monitors indicated that she still had a lot of brain activity. The doctor explained that brain surgery was needed, but "her body is suffering withdrawals from her nicotine addiction, making surgery more dangerous." The doctor said that my mama may never wake up, or she could wake up at any moment.

The family that was gathered there was speechless. I was in shock, and assume others were also. When the doctor left us, we took our seats in the waiting room, mostly remaining silent. We were in disbelief. Hours passed. Later that night, we agreed someone should remain there in the waiting room to alert the others if she were to regain consciousness. Ray agreed to take the first night shift, giving the rest of us temporary relief from the sterile hospital environment.

The doctor reported the following day there had been no changes in mama's condition overnight and instructed us to be prepared for her condition to remain unchanged for days and possibly for weeks. Catherine was in her sixth month of pregnancy so the waiting room for the Intensive Care Unit was barely tolerable for her. I took her and Bailey home to Madison, and promptly returned to the hospital. Upon my return, the prognosis was unchanged and remained unchanged for the rest of the week. The family discussed the possibility that she might get better care in a larger hospital in Mobile or New Orleans, but the doctor said that she was too unstable to be transported and too unstable to operate. According to the doctor, if she became stable, they could operate so there would be no need to transport her.

There was not a moment when I accepted the possibility that she might not recover. She was a strong woman and relatively young. In my mind, she would have a full recovery and things would return, as they were, so I made the decision to go home and return to work after getting assurance from those who remained, they would call me immediately if there were any changes in her condition. Within a day or two later, I got a call that my mama had awakened from her coma. Catherine and I traveled from Madison to Pascagoula in record time, as if we were in a flying car.

The medical practitioner on duty informed us that we could enter the room no more than two at a time. My heart fluttered with excitement. I could hardly believe my ears. We could enter her room two at a time, so my sister and I entered the room together. Mama was awake, but she was on so many drugs that she was not lucid. She was hallucinating. She laughed and giggled because she thought there was "a man over there by the door wearing a tiger suit. He thinks that I don't see him, but I do. Tell him that I know that he is there," she would say with laughter. "He thinks he is fooling me, but I know that he is not a real tiger. He is just a man in a tiger suit. Tell him that I know his trick," she said to me.

When my time was up, I left the room extraordinarily frustrated. On the one hand, I was pleased to see her in good spirits, and laughing, but was disappointed because we couldn't have a meaningful conversation, and there were so many things

I wanted to say to her. I was encouraged by her having awakened because it gave me hope she would wake up again.

Starlie regained consciousness for the second time in mid-January, and she wasn't hallucinating this time. But she was worse than incoherent, this time she was terrified. I could feel her trembling with fear as I held her hand and asked what was wrong. With teary eyes and a crying voice, she said, "I killed my daddy." She repeated it again, over, and over. My heart sank. She spoke to me only once about the tragic event, when I was twelve, which was over twenty years prior.

***

I recalled the night my stepbrother and I heard her summon us from our beds. "There is something important I need to tell you." She spoke to both of us but looked mostly at me. She looked directly into my eyes and said, "What I must tell you is not something I am proud of... but I am not ashamed of it either. This is something you need to hear from me. You are now old enough to hear this, and it's best you hear this from me and not from someone else." She had never been so dramatic before, creating anxiety as I waited to hear this important message. "After I tell you what it is that I have to say, you can ask me any questions you have about it just this one time... but after tonight, we are never to discuss this again. Do you understand and agree?'

We both nodded in agreement.

"Years ago…" She paused before continuing, searching for the words. "Long before you were born, I killed my daddy." She paused for several seconds to allow us to process her words. Our wide-eyed expression let her know we had.

"Had you heard about this before tonight?" she asked.

We both answered truthfully, "no" while shaking our heads to reiterate our answers. She was surprised and even asked again as if she couldn't believe that no one had ever told either of us. She even specifically asked if we had heard that from Earline or her children. Aunt Earline, as I knew her, lived next door to us in Pascagoula, with her three children. In retrospect, I think that she was afraid that Earline's oldest child, Cecil might tell us. He was a couple of years older than I, and Starlie may have learned that Cecil knew.

"Well, if that is true, then you are probably wondering why I killed my daddy."

We both nodded, still in shock from hearing this traumatic news.

"My daddy was a very bad man. He did terrible things to me and to my mother, and to Earline too." She explained how he was suspected of killing people. She told us the story about the man who went fishing with her daddy after playing cards all night, never to be seen again, and how he made Anna Mae wash the blood from the missing man's clothes. She told us the details of that fateful night when Ernest threatened to kill David. Looking directly into my eyes she said, "I want you to know that I love you more than I love my own life. Do you recall the many times that I told you that I would throw myself in front of a moving train or bus if that was what it took to save your life?"

I nodded.

"Well, I meant that when I said it. I *would* through myself in front of a moving train or take a bullet meant for you. If a man with a knife or gun were trying to harm you, I would put myself in between you to save you, or any of my children for that matter. One day, hopefully, you will have children of your own, and you will know what it is like to love someone more than your own life."

She paused for a moment to add emphasis to her next words, "If I am willing to die to save your life, do you think it's reasonable that I would be willing to end someone else's life if that was the only way to save your life?"

That made perfect sense to me, and I let her know it. We both nodded.

She continued. "If someone came into this house tonight and threatened you, I would do whatever it took to save you, even if that meant sacrificing my life. But, given the choice, I would rather sacrifice the life of the person trying to harm you, than to sacrifice my own life. Do you agree with that?"

Of course, I did.

"That is the choice I had to make that terrible night, long ago, before you were born. My choice was to either kill my own daddy or allow him to kill my baby son, David, and me, and mama, and your daddy. I knew that he was capable of it, and I knew that he would likely kill the rest of my family too.

"Why?" I asked, "Why did he want to kill David?"

"He was mad at us because Earline reported him to the police for something bad, he did, and when he got out of jail, he found out that Charles and I had run away with mama, trying to get away from him. He tracked us down and found where we were hiding. He was drinking a lot, cursing, and threatening us. He drank so much that he passed out, but the last thing he said before passing out was *I'm going to kill that little bastard when I wake up first thing*. I knew that he meant it too."

Mama's chin quivered. Having to relive the nightmare by telling her son, must have been a horrendous experience for her. Speaking slowly, she continued. "It wasn't a difficult decision. I knew right then - as soon as he said those words - what I had to do. I knew that my daddy could never wake up from that sleep. My mother was there, and we talked it over, and together we agreed that my daddy had to die to save David's life, so I took a shotgun that was in the house; I loaded it, and then I aimed it at my daddy's head while he lay there asleep. Then I pulled the trigger, and he was dead."

I could see her reliving the horror as she spoke.

"I pray I never have to make such a decision again, and I pray you never have to make a similar decision. But you need to know I would make the same choice if I had to do it again. It was the only choice I had."

She paused briefly.

"It is important you understand I do not condone violence, and it is not ok to kill anyone ever unless it is to save a life. I've told you many times, always walk away from a fight if you can, but if you can't walk away; if you are backed into a corner and have no choice but to fight, then fight as if your life depends on it because it just might."

"It's also important for you to know also just because my daddy was a bad man, you don't have to be ashamed of who you are. You are not responsible for the sins of your father or your ancestors. He does not define you, no one does for that matter, other than you. You and you alone determine who and what you are. It doesn't matter how you got here; it matters what you do with the time God has given you. Never forget that."

"Now, do you have any questions for me?"

We may have asked a few questions, I honestly can't remember, but she concluded by reminding us "after tonight, I don't want either one of you to bring this up again to me or to anyone else. If someone else brings this up to you, tell them 'Yes I know about that and don't want to talk about it' and say no more about this to anyone, out of respect for me. Do you understand how this is not something I want anyone talking about?"

We n ever discussed that terrible, life-altering event again, until she was lying on her deathbed in Singing River Hospital, twenty-two years later.

***

I held her hand and tried to calm her but to no avail. I couldn't think of anything to say other than, "It's all right."

But she responded with a resounding, "No! It's not all right. God says thou shalt not kill and I killed my daddy!"

"Mama, God, and everyone else understands you had no choice. You did what you had to do to save the family. I would not be here if you hadn't saved our family," I said. My heart was breaking because I couldn't calm her fears, no matter what I said.

My time expired, so I left the room overwhelmed with emotion. No one was able to calm her, so the Doctors gave her more medicine to calm her, but it made her fall back into a coma.

Returning to my spot in the waiting area, I realized she might not recover. My heart ached beyond imagination at the thought my mother might leave this world frightened. I prayed for a different ending for her. For the first time in my life, I began to realize how profoundly and permanently she had been affected by the abuse and torture she suffered. I remembered how she avoided all social events, hiding in the back row, and trying to be unnoticed at all of my school events. Her self-esteem never fully recovered. She spent very little money on herself, thinking she was unworthy of nice clothes or an expensive hairstyle. She felt as if people looked at her and thought poorly of her and was concerned her children would be looked upon as "poor white trash" because of her actions.

Mama was aware there is no statute of limitations for murder, and Ernest's sisters petitioned the court several times over the years to have charges filed against her. She feared most of all the publicity would bring shame to her family. She desperately wanted to spare her children from embarrassment. I regret never having told her how proud I was of her. Mama loved seeing her children enjoying a normal life, going to school, attending proms and parties, playing ball, having friends, and having a stable home life. She may have worried the past would rear its ugly head, and she would once again be in the news for killing her father. Her concern was mostly for her children. She feared we would be embarrassed, ostracized, and our normal life would be over. This may be why my mother suffered from chronic ulcers and depression.

Sitting in the waiting room for hours gave me time to reflect. I recalled the last quality visit I had with Mama. She drove from Pascagoula to Madison to visit her newborn grandson, Bailey during his first Christmas holiday a little more than a year ago. I remember her smile with joy at the sight of me gently rubbing Bailey's forehead as he lay on my chest. She said to me, "I cannot express how happy it is to see that you are gentle with your baby."

Not having thought about her childhood experiences for many years, her statement was peculiar at the time. I replied, "Who could possibly be mean to a baby?"

"Not everyone is kind. Some people can be mean, even to babies."

While sitting in the waiting room, reflecting, I finally understood her concern. She may have observed me over the years, wondering if I might have an evil side like her father. Like most teenage boys with overflowing testosterone, I probably said things to sound tougher than I really was which may have caused her concern. I closed my eyes and tried to think as far back into my memory as I could, trying to see if I could recall the overlooked clues she had provided regarding her lingering torment from that dreadful night.

***

The vision of a small, pale green house with asbestos siding and a flat roof appeared. My first home was located on Charles Street, named in honor of my father because he was the first to live on the street. It had a shell drive and was enclosed by a chain-linked fence.

Immediately after the Houston authorities completed their investigation and decided not to file charges against Starlie, she and Charles moved to Mobile where they lived with Charles' mother and father. Shortly thereafter, Charles got a job working for International Paper Company in Moss Point, Mississippi.

The story Charles liked to tell was about the day of his hiring. He stood in line with the other job applicants waiting for his name to be called. Dozens of names were called over a bullhorn, and a hand would be raised in the air. "Ok, you are hired, move to this side," the man with the bullhorn would say. Sometimes a name would be called two times and no hand would be raised, so the announcer would say, "Last chance...ok, next," and then he would call a different name. When the announcer got to the last name, they called out twice and when Charles realized that no one else was going to raise a hand, he raised his hand and murmured, "I will be him if that is what it takes to get the job." Not hearing his confession and assuming he was the person they called out for, he was signaled to step forward and instructed to complete his hiring paperwork. He worked there for forty-four years until he retired at age sixty-five.

Charles never graduated from high school, was married at seventeen, and a father by age eighteen. But he had a strong work ethic and was committed to supporting his family. He and my mother had four children: David, who was Ernest's intended victim; Peggy who died of cystic fibrosis when she was only four years of age; Wanda, who was born four years after David; and their fourth and final child, me, Darryl.

Lacking a formal education beyond the tenth grade meant he had to start at the bottom of the paper mill's workforce hierarchy and would never work his way up much higher with the company. Nevertheless, my dad was innovative. He purchased "scrub pine land" for $5000 and sold off parcels of his cheap land to others to afford that flat-roofed home in Moss Point. He also purchased other homes for rental income and worked a sales route on his off days, selling wigs and Old Spice products.

My father taught me a work ethic and commitment to family, but my mother raised me. She also had a strong work ethic, sometimes working a day job and a night job, and she was the wisest and least selfish woman that I've ever personally known.

Once when I was about to begin school, she took me to the paper mill where my father worked. The mill hosted an annual open house day for workers' families. This was a chance for families to see where their father or mother worked and what they did for a living. I recall the sweltering heat, and the smell of the papermill was so foul that I thought I was going to vomit. When my dad saw us, a big smile flashed across his face, and he put down the broom he was using to sweep the concrete floor. He rushed over to us. I couldn't hear a word he was saying because the roaring sound of the machines, whistles, and boilers was deafening. I started to remove my earplugs so I could understand what he was trying to say, but he stopped me and shook his head, so I knew not to remove the earplugs.

Afterward, my mother drove her Oldsmobile to the bank with me riding along beside her in the front seat, my window open so I could stick my head out to feel the wind on my face. This was long before seat belt laws. Many cars didn't even have seat belts. We didn't go to the neighborhood branch as was the norm. This time she made a special trip to the bank's headquarters in downtown Pascagoula. I don't recall ever going there with her before or since. The sudden blast of cool, conditioned air was a huge relief from the sweltering heat that only those of us in the deep South can truly appreciate. Once inside the bank, she stopped at a counter to fill out a deposit slip.

"It feels good in here, doesn't it?" she asked. I nodded. She picked me up and put me on the counter so that I was eye to eye with her. "Do you know why it feels so good in here?"

"No, ma'am."

"It's because this room is air-conditioned. Do you remember how hot it was at the paper mill where your father works?"

"Yes, ma'am."

"Do you remember how loud and hot it was where your father worked?"

"Yes, and it stinks there too!"

"Do you see the man over there?" She subtly directed my attention to a man sitting behind a nice desk behind a glass wall. "Look at the man over there. Notice how he is wearing nice clothes, sitting in a chair, talking on the telephone in an air-conditioned office that doesn't stink? Instead of having to wear earplugs all day, he listens to music playing in the background."

I hadn't noticed the music before or given much thought to the people around me and what they did for a living, until that moment.

"What kind of job would you rather have when you grow up? Would you rather work in a hot, loud, and smelly place, sweeping floors and working all hours of the day and night, or would you rather have a job like a man over there? He is home every night and every weekend with his family, and would you believe that he makes more money than your father does?"

Even at a young age, I was able to answer that question correctly.

"Do you know the difference between the man over there, why he has such a good job, and your father, who has a hard job which doesn't pay well?" Before I could answer, she told me, "It's because the man over there went to college and got a good education, and your father and I never had the opportunity to get an education – but you do."

She gave me a few minutes for her message to sink in and continued to explain to me, "you can go to college one day and have a good job, if you make good choices, make good grades in school, and stay out of trouble, but it won't be easy."

"If you decide when you are young to stay in school, make good grades, and stay out of trouble, you won't have to work as hard for the rest of your life, but if you choose to goof off and flunk out of school, you will pay for it for the rest of your life by having to work a hard job for little pay."

At the time, I didn't know what a college was, but I knew it was important and I wanted to go there. She often reminded me over the years. My mind jumped to the time when I was in high school, and it had become apparent that playing football allowed me the only opportunity to get a college education.

I recall my mother telling me once before a game, "I want you to pretend every time that ball is snapped, a college football coach is watching you and that very play is your job interview because it might very well be that way. You never know who is watching you and one play might mean the difference between getting a scholarship or not. The same is true if you decide to loaf on the very play someone important is watching, and if you are caught loafing, well, just remember, there is another boy who is on the sideline watching you, waiting for his chance."

Although she knew almost nothing about football, she knew how important it was to my future. For that reason, she was at every single home football game, cheering me on.

My mind drifted back in time to the first day of the second grade. That was the first year that public schools in that part of Mississippi were forced to integrate. Like a lot of parents, my parents kept me at home for the first two weeks of school, but I was unaware school had started.

My best friend at the time was Freddie. He lived across the street and was two years older, but only one grade ahead of me in school. I spent a lot of time at Freddie's house. He was a smart kid who loved science and history. His father gave him a set of encyclopedias for kids called the Knowledge Books. Freddie would constantly educate me about something new; first dinosaurs, then planets, then sharks, then whatever.

Robbie was another neighborhood kid who was often hanging out with us at Freddie's house. I first learned I was missing school from Robbie.

"Are your parents making you go to school with n----s?" Robbie asked.

I had never heard that word, so I responded, "I don't know. What are n----s?"

"You don't know what a n----r is?" He laughed. "They are black kids, like those who live on the other side of Pine Island Boulevard."

"Black? What do you mean black kids?" I was perplexed. I had no idea what he was talking about.

Freddie pulled out one of his comic books and showed me a frame of the comic hero, the Black Panther, with his mask removed and said, "This is what a black person looks like."

I had seen the Black Panther without his mask, but I never paid any attention to the fact he had black skin, because all of the comic characters looked different – the Thing from the Fantastic Four had rocks for skin, the Torch was flames, the Hulk was green, and so on.

"Haven't you ever noticed black people when your mama takes you to the grocery store?" Robbie asked.

I thought for a moment. I hadn't noticed and felt foolish because Robbie was laughing at my naiveté, so I lied and said I had noticed.

Fast forward many years later, around 2012. A good friend wanted a child, but as she approached fifty years of age, hadn't found her soul mate. So, she decided to adopt a beautiful little girl who happens to be of African descent. One night while I was visiting, she put her little girl to bed, and said to me; "She is nearly six years old, and she hasn't said anything to me about the fact we have a different skin color. I expect she will come home one day and ask me why we look different." Her little girl was just as oblivious to skin color as I was at her age. Maybe if grown-ups didn't make a big deal about it, kids wouldn't either, and one day, no one would give skin color a second thought.

Back in the Sixties

A little while later, when it was time for bed, I asked my mother if I had to go to school with n----rs, and she asked me how I had heard that word. I told her, and she explained to me that was a bad word and not to say it again. Then she tried to put my mind at ease about going to school with black kids. I remember vividly that she said, "Always remember, that no matter how different people seem at first, they have more things in common than differences. For example, almost every little boy has a mother who loves him, as I love you, and almost every mother wants the best for their children, and if you remember that, you will know we aren't so different after all."

Her words helped me sleep better that night, but my anxiety reappeared the next morning when it was time to get into the car to go to school. My mother, brother, and sister escorted me to the car where my father was already behind the wheel.

"Ok, time to get in the car. We must go if we aren't going to be late," my father called out.

That is when panic set in. I remember, embarrassingly, that I fought hard to resist getting in that car. I stretched out my arms and spread my legs as wide as possible so that they could not put me in the car. I screamed bloody murder, "NO! NO! DON'T MAKE ME GO TO SCHOOL WITH N-----S!"

I was terrified of people with whom I had been around my whole, short life yet had never noticed them before, thanks to Robbie, who passed the anxiety on from his father or older brothers. I lost the battle and went to school. I will never forget the first day of the second grade. My mother walked me to the school door to make certain that I didn't run off. I remember looking around to see if I saw any black kids. Once seated in my classroom, I looked around, and there *they* were, black kids. I didn't want them to see me looking, so I kept my head facing forward as much as I could, pupils in the corner of my eyes trying to watch them. I remember catching the eye of a black classmate, and we both quickly looked away, each afraid to make eye contact. He was just as anxious about me as I was about him. In retrospect, had no one ever said anything to either one of us about race, we would not likely have given one another a thought. We would have been like my friend's little girl, oblivious to our differences.

After the first few days, I believe we all became accustomed to one another, and I don't recall ever having a confrontation with any black students throughout the remainder of my school life. I say significant because there were a couple of times when I squared off to fight, but the color of our skin had no role in the situation. I squared off to fight white kids more often than I did with black kids. That's what kids did back then; we fought from time to time. But we forgot our differences as soon as the fight was over. The fight settled our differences. The concern about race faded, as far as I could tell.

The following summer exposed me to a traumatic event. There were no indications my parents were having troubles, as far as I could tell, until the night Starlie left Charles, taking Wanda and me with her. They never told me why they divorced, but I suspect Starlie harbored resentment towards Charles for her having to pull the trigger to take her father's life to protect their child, and not him.

Starlie rented a house just a few miles away and I was given a choice as to whom I wanted to live with. My father told me that he would do the best he could to raise me, but "I work all of the time and I can't cook." My mother told me that she would bake pies for me whenever I like. I love pies.

My sister and I lived with my mother but my brother was

already married and had a home of his own. That summer was difficult. We didn't have an air-conditioner, and it gets very hot in Mississippi. My mother worked day and night and she still didn't make enough money to keep the electricity from being turned off a time or two. The water may have been turned off once or twice also. I recall asking my mother for a new bicycle for my birthday and she said "No, son. I wish that I could afford it, but I can't."

"Why can't we afford a bicycle? Everyone else has one," I asked.

"Because we are poor, that's why," she answered.

Years later, a relative said that "Being poor is a state of mind. I've been broke many times, but I've never been poor." I subscribe to that theory.

My new best friend at the time lived in a nearby housing project where every home looked identical. I envied his home because every home was bricked, and ours was wood, lap siding, with so much paint missing that the home looked as if it had freckles. My buddy asked me if I wanted to play baseball. His dad was a coach. I asked what I had to do to be on the team. I needed a pair of cleats and a glove, but my buddy told me he had an extra glove for me, so all that I needed was a pair of cleats. I ran home as fast as I could to plead with my mother to buy a pair of cleats for me to play baseball.

"No, honey, I am sorry, but I cannot afford cleats. Did you forget? We're poor."

Saddened by the answer, I return to tell my friend that I could not play because we could not afford cleats.

His eyes lit up. "I know where a pair of cleats is! Follow me!" He led me to a garbage dumpster, reached in, and pulled out a discarded pair of old worn-out baseball cleats. I tried them on. They were at least one size too small, and the cleats were worn to a nub, but I really wanted to play baseball. I ran home to show my mother that I had cleats. She saw that they were too small and worn out, and she told me "I'm sorry son, but you cannot wear those cleats."

"Why, Mama? I don't care if they are too small. I want to play baseball."

"Son, you can play baseball when I can afford to buy you a pair of cleats, but you aren't going to wear someone's discarded cleats that you dug out of the garbage. We aren't poor white trash."

"We aren't poor?" I asked.

"No, we aren't."

"Great! Can I have a bicycle?"

As the summer ended, my mother informed me she was getting remarried and that we were all moving to Pascagoula to live with our new family. I didn't know what to think about this new concept of having a stepfamily.

Darryl R. Breland

Chapter 4: Coming Together

Norvell had just survived the longest and most treacherous day of his life. He had not expected to survive the invasion of Sword Beach, but now he and the rest of his unit witnessed the last of enemy gunfire from within the heart of Paris. People began cheering from windows and balconies. More people began filling the streets and sidewalks, waving and cheering. He wanted to celebrate the victory as well, but his legs were still shaking, adrenalin still flowing from having the prospect of sudden death haunting him all day long. With great apprehension, he stood, fully exposed to potential enemy gunfire for the first time that day.

Women and children charged toward him and his mates, arms stretched wide, tears flowing, and sporting grateful smiles. The first woman that embraced him was much older than his age of thirty-four and twice his weight. She grabbed his face and tried to plant a kiss on his lips, but his instincts caused him to turn his face so that her kiss landed on his cheek. She said, "merci mille fois" and then unclenched him, grabbed another British soldier, and repeated the process. No sooner had she let go of Norvell, than another ecstatic Frenchwoman did the same. Children hugged his legs. Old men tried to get close enough to show their gratitude for liberating their city from the Nazi nightmare. He and his troops could hardly advance due to the swelling mob of Parisians. Then suddenly everything felt different.

The body that had currently embraced him was not that of an old, overweight woman. He had only a glimpse of her face before her lips reached his, but that was enough to keep him from turning his cheek. This was a real kiss. With eyes closed and arms wrapped around one another, they both felt each other's bodies and knew that they were a perfect fit. They ignored the other women who tried to separate them to take their turn in thanking the liberator and continued the longest kiss. When they stopped kissing, they remained in each other's arms and examined each other's faces. She was the most beautiful woman that Norvell had ever seen. She must have felt the same about him because everything froze in time around them. They no longer heard the cheering crowds. Without saying a word, they gazed into one another's eyes, each instantly believing that they both knew what the other was thinking – you are the one.

They slowly relaxed their embrace, making certain to become separated by the mob by clinging to one another's arms and holding hands, he led her to the quietest and most secluded spot on the street without losing sight of his army unit. He tried to introduce himself, but he did not speak French, and she did not speak English. He looked around and saw what he needed through the window of the corner store next to where they stood. He led her inside and picked up a writing pen and tore a piece of paper from the billing pad which rested on the clerk's counter. He handed her the pen and paper and said, "Please write your name and where I can find you." He then tore another sheet from the pad and wrote his name, rank, and the words:

I will return for you on the first Christmas Day after Hitler is defeated.

She may not have understood everything he said, but she knew enough to write her name, Caroline, and address.

Earlier that day, Norvell was pinned down by enemy gunfire. Soldiers all around him were falling to the ground, wounded, or dead. He truly thought that he would not survive the day. He began to reflect on his life and his family. He had never married before. Not that he was opposed to the idea; he just had never met the one. He truly wanted an opportunity to return home, as it was before the war, settle down and have a family of his own. He may have made a pact with God that morning because he did survive the war, and he did return to his hometown in England – with Caroline.

He had been a welder at a shipyard before the war, but his government wasn't investing in shipbuilding anymore, but the United States was, and in a big way. One of the biggest shipyards in the world at that time was in Pascagoula, Mississippi, so

Norvell and his bride moved to the tiny but rapidly growing town that neither of them could pronounce. Not long after moving to Pascagoula, Patricia was born. She was their only child. Norvell and Caroline lived happily ever after, together for the rest of their long lives, in Pascagoula.

Patricia grew up and married a local boy named Ray Vice. Norvell and Caroline may not have approved of Ray initially, considering that Vice is a German surname, but more importantly, there was a local criminal gang of Vices with very bad reputations.

America was experiencing tumultuous times in the 1950s and 1960s. In response to the Civil Rights Movement, a domestic terrorist organization, the Ku Klux Klan, or KKK, had resurrected itself. Criminal organizations formed a nationwide network known as the Mafia which affected nearly every city and town. The criminal organization on the Mississippi Gulf Coast at that time was known as the Dixie Mafia. We learned later that the Mississippi Gulf Coast was also the territory of the New Orleans-based Sicilian Mafioso, Carlos Marcello.

A reputed hitman for the Dixie Mafia, allegedly, was Coda Lloyd Vice, a cousin to Ray.

Coda Lloyd and his brothers were known infamously as the Vice Gang. Whether or not the rumors were true that they were connected to the Mafia or performed deadly services on behalf of the KKK, we may never know for sure, but we *do* know that they were suspected of many crimes including several murders, and Coda Lloyd *was* eventually convicted of murder.

Ray was not like his violent cousins. He was a gentle and kind man, a law-abiding citizen committed to doing the right thing. He, like my father, did not have a formal education but had a virtual life-long career as a paper mill worker. He and Patricia had three children.

Norvell and Caroline lived happily ever after, together for the rest of their lives, but Patricia and Ray did not. They divorced in the summer of 1968, the same summer that my mother and father divorced. About a year later, my mother and Ray were married.

Ray was embarrassed by his criminal cousins and felt as if his name was stained by their reputations. No one could understand how he felt more than my mother.

My oldest brother had already married and had a home of his own, so Starlie, my sister, and I moved into Ray's home in Pascagoula. Ray's three children lived there as well. We got along well enough, but we certainly weren't the Brady Bunch.

Our new home was small and crowded. The "carport" had

been enclosed to serve as a third bedroom, which I shared with my two stepbrothers. The walls were thin wood panels over studs. A few years later, wall insulation was added.

My younger stepbrother was eight months younger than I. My other stepbrother was seven years older. My new stepsister shared her bedroom with my sister, Wanda. There was only one bathroom in the entire house, which meant that we had to stand in line to take a bath. The bathroom had only a toilet and a tub. There was not a showerhead at first, so bathing in the tub was the only option.

The floors were bare concrete throughout the entire house, except for a small patch of asphalt tiles in the kitchen area. There was no carpet, ceramic, or hardwood flooring. I recall visiting a classmate who had wall-to-wall carpet and concluding that anyone who had carpet must be rich. The living room was cooled by a single window unit. There was also a window unit in the master bedroom.

Feeding such a big family was quite a burden for Mama and Ray. We ate a lot of French fries and fish sticks and lots of rice and beans. One night we would have red beans and rice. The next night we would have lima beans and rice. The next night, my mother would serve us mashed lima beans and rice so we would think that we were having something new for dinner. The truth is, we didn't always eat beans and rice. Sometimes we ate peanut butter or corn dogs. On special occasions, my mother, being from south Texas, would cook the best Tex-Mex dishes – enchiladas, quesadillas, and homemade tacos were her specialty. And, being Southerners, we often ate fried chicken, and being near the Gulf we ate our fair share of fish and shrimp.

Our small house was so close to the Gulf of Mexico we could walk there. We could even see the water from our backyard. One day, my stepbrother and I took my stepfather's casting net to the beach. We waded out into the water and cast the net for hours, slowly but surely filling our bucket with shrimp. We were so proud of ourselves for the whole family had shrimp creole for dinner that night. I was eight years old, and that was the first time I fed a family, with my younger stepbrother's help. In fact, it may have been his idea.

We had hardly gotten to know each other when disaster struck. On August 14, 1969, my mother started yelling in a panic for all of us to gather as much as we could fit in one bag and get into the car as quickly as we could. My mother drove the green station wagon, adorned with faux wood panels on the exterior of the car doors, loaded with five children to pick up my stepfather who was at the paper mill where he worked. The hurricane had stalled just off the Mississippi Coast for days and had made its move – due north toward our home. There were only two hours before the eye of the most powerful storm in recorded history was to make landfall. The roads were jammed with cars trying to escape. We could feel the wind shaking our car violently as we waited in slow-moving traffic. I recall Ray whispering to my mother. "I sure hope that we aren't still in this car when the hurricane arrives."

We returned a couple of weeks later to a house that was virtually a total loss. The floors were covered, four inches deep, in mud. There was no electricity or running water. Cleaning up and rebuilding was a family effort, and it was hard work. The August weather in the deepest of the Deep South made conditions worse. Unless you've experienced the wrath of a hurricane, there is no way to truly imagine the magnitude of destruction. I remember that I was feeling overwhelmed, so I took a break from cleaning, walked outside, and rested against the telephone pole that was on the corner of our property.

My mother followed me outside. She must have sensed my despair. "I realize that times are tough, and things seem gloomy," she said, "but better times are ahead. Don't give up."

Chapter 5: Saying Goodbye

Despite all the challenges that she had experienced in life, she was still an optimist. It just did not seem right that after she had spent a lifetime caring for and protecting others, she now faced the possibility of dying without experiencing the many things that she had looked forward to doing when she was "retired."

After seeing her so frightened to meet her maker, I worried that she might not ever leave the hospital alive. Then I thought about all the times that I was so insensitive to her. Not knowing that she deserved only kindness and consideration. I thought about how many times I was an absolute jerk to her. I prayed for an opportunity to talk to her one more time so that I could tell her that I now understood her.

A few days later, my prayers were answered. She awoke from her coma, one final time. She was alert this time. She wasn't hallucinating, she wasn't frightened. She had a clear head, and I was able to tell her that she need not be frightened because God understands and forgives her. She smiled, and said, "I know Darryl. I am not afraid any longer." Then she went on to tell me that she saw our baby, which hadn't been born yet. "She is a beautiful girl."

There is a legend that a Pascagoula Indian hooked up with the daughter of the Biloxi Indian's chief, and he was so pissed, that war on Pascagoula was declared. Pascagoula Indians, being lovers and not fighters, committed mass suicide by drowning themselves in the Pascagoula River, singing as they went to their deaths, rather than face the wrath of the larger and more fierce Biloxi Indians. On warm summer nights, people have heard a low humming sound coming from the river, especially after a few drinks. In any event, it's a good excuse to park in a romantic spot alongside the river. Nowadays, Pascagoula is known as the Singing River City, hence the name of the hospital.

"That's amazing, Mama because we haven't told anyone. You will be happy to know that we are naming her Anna in honor of your mother Anna Mae."

My mother was pleased.

"Mama, there is something else that I need to tell you..." I then got very emotional and had a hard time getting the words to come out, but I managed to tell her that I was so sorry for all the times that I treated her poorly. I thank God Almighty for that opportunity because I don't believe that I would have been able to forgive myself had I not told her that before she passed.

Being the sweet mother she was, she smiled and said, "Don't you worry son, I love you and you've been a very good son."

> *It is easier to build up a child than repair an adult. Your words and actions have power in your child's life, use them wisely!*
>
> *~ Author Unknown*

Telling this story wasn't easy for me, but I believe my grandchildren and their grandchildren need to know the truth about my mother, Starlie. One of my next books will be on the History of the Breland Family. While researching my family history, I learned things about my ancestors, and it occurred to me that one day one of Starlie's descendants might uncover news reports about her while researching our family. I would rather they know the truth rather than speculate or wonder what happened that terrible night.

PART TWO:

Starlie's Legacy

Darryl R. Breland

Chapter 6: Tina

Tina gently placed her infant son, Jamie, in his baby bed before answering the telephone. It was the life insurance agent, calling from his car phone to inform her that he had entered her apartment complex. "Ok, I will step outside so that you can see which apartment is mine," she said.

The agent parked his black BMW convertible in front of Tina's apartment, where she was standing, opened his car door, and said, "Hi, Mrs. Collins, how are you today?"

Tina displayed one of her infectious smiles and replied, "It's *Miss* Collins, but you may call me Tina."

"Oh, I just assumed that Peter Boyette is your husband since he is named as your beneficiary," said the agent as he closed his car door and approached Tina with his brief in one hand, and a business card in the other.

"No problem, most people assume that. Peter is my baby's daddy, and we live together, but we are not married yet," she said in her customary friendly manner.

"I see. Well, I am Buddy Thomas, your insurance agent, and I have your life insurance policy. Just need your John Hancock in a couple of spots."

"Come on in." She directed him to sit at the breakfast table in her modest apartment. "Just try not to wake the baby," she said holding her finger to her lips. "Would you care for some tea?"

"Yes, much appreciated," he said following her instructions to sit. "As we discussed before, you were approved for a $250,000 life insurance policy, which pays double in the event of an accident claim. Please look this over and sign here and here, then initial these pages."

Tina flipped through the pages of the contract and began signing where the agent had placed checkmarks, and remarked, "Peter is the one that knows more about this than I do, but if this is as y'all agreed, here you go."

"Thank you, I truly appreciate your business," he said.

They stood, and as she opened the door, she replied "You're welcome." She stepped outside with the agent as he opened the door to his car. "That's a really nice car. What year is it?"

"Thanks! It's a 2004 model. Just bought it. Still has that new car smell," he said, beaming with pride.

"Wow, they've already come out with next year's models?"

"Yep, next year's models come out this time each year."

"Selling life insurance must be lucrative."

"It can be, once you're established, but it can be tough at the beginning. You would be good at this, with your friendly personality and all. You should get your license."

"Thanks, you're nice to say that, but I'm not a salesperson."

"Don't sell yourself short. No pun intended." He chuckled. "You can be anything that you want if you put your mind to it." He opened his car door and slid behind the wheel. The car was started, and he lowered the window before closing the door so that he could continue to talk with Tina, who had followed him to his car.

"Oh, by the way, do you have Peter's life insurance policy? I know you'll need a signature on his as well, but he's ok if I sign for him, if that's okay with you."

The agent paused for a second, and then answered, "No, Peter didn't apply for a policy with me. He told me that he already had coverage with another company. Do I need to run a quote for him?"

That was a surprise to her. Peter was adamant that they both obtain a life insurance policy now that they had a new baby.

With a quizzical expression, Tina asked, "Did he say which company that he bought his policy from?"

The agent, somewhat suspicious that Peter hadn't been honest with either of them, "He told me he had a policy with Blue Cross and Blue Shield…but when I told him that they don't sell life insurance, then he said he thought it might be with State Farm. I thought it odd that he couldn't remember."

"That's weird. This was his idea, for us to get life insurance."

"It *is* unusual not to remember the name of your life insurance company…I offered to compare our rates to his current policy, but he said he was good." The agent was encouraged that another sale may be on the horizon.

"Well, I'll talk to him when he gets home, and if we need to, we will call you back to write a policy on him as well."

With that, the agent lowered his convertible top and drove away. Tina went inside her apartment and called her father, Paul, who was in his backyard workshop organizing his tools. Today was his day off from work, but he isn't a man who can sit still.

"Hi Dad, what are you doing?"

"Same thing that I was doing the last time we talked,

organizing my workshop, trying to eliminate so much clutter. What's up?"

"My life insurance agent just delivered my policy, so I'm covered if something happens to me."

"Okay, congratulations."

"I'm a little confused about something, though," she said, wondering how she can tell her father of her concerns without sounding accusatory or suspicious of the man she considered to be her husband. She knew how her father didn't approve of Peter, and she didn't want to give him another reason to not like him.

"What is it? Didn't the agent explain how it all works? You die, and your beneficiary gets a check. What else is there to know?"

"Oh, never mind, its nothing," she said, reconsidering whether it was wise to involve her father before talking to Peter.

"What is it, darling? I didn't mean to be rude," Paul said.

"It's nothing really. I've to go now, Jamie needs me. Talk to you later."

"Okay, if you need me, my phone is in my pocket at all times." Paul sensed that something was concerning her.

"I know, Dad. I love you. Bye for now."

"I love you, too, sweetheart, bye."

Jamie was in his stroller, playing with a toy rattle, when Tina heard Peter's motorcycle as he approached the parking space near their front door. She was sitting on the sofa when he entered the apartment. He hardly acknowledged Tina when he entered. Holding his cell phone to his ear with one hand he dropped his motorcycle helmet and backpack on the closest chair and rushed up the stairs, appearing to be engaged in his telephone call the entire time.

A short time later, Peter's loud footsteps could be heard, as he rushed down the stairs. He went straight to the kitchen and opened the refrigerator. "Is there anything in here to eat? I'm starving," he asked.

"Not much. It's hard to go to the grocery store with a six-month-old baby, and even harder with no money…Oh, and hello! How was your day, also?" She replied with a hint of sarcasm.

"I just gave you thirty bucks, what did you do with that money?"

"That was a week ago. I had to buy baby formula and gas for my car. Thirty dollars doesn't go very far."

"Shit. I guess we'll have another pizza...*again*."

Later, when they sat down for dinner, she handed him his plate full of pizza slices. "What are we going to do for Halloween? It's this coming weekend, you know."

Speaking with a mouth full of pizza, he said, "There will be a killer band playing on campus at one of the frat houses." Then he took a swig of beer. "I think that would be fun."

"Have you forgotten that we have a baby?" She asked.

"No, I haven't forgotten. Do you think that I'm stupid? Let's get a babysitter."

"How can we afford a babysitter if we can't afford groceries?"

"I don't fucking know! Shit! We can't ever do anything fun anymore. What do you want to do? Stay home and give candy to trick-or-treaters?"

Peter was volatile and could easily fly into a rage. Tina was no pushover, but she knew his screaming rages were upsetting to the baby. She didn't like it either, but she didn't want to provoke him for the baby's sake.

In a tone intended to calm, she replied, "Yes, that's exactly what I have in mind. It'll be Jamie's first Halloween, so we should spend it with him. Wouldn't it be cute to see him dressed up in his first costume?"

"Lame," Peter replied.

"Well, you can go to the party if you want, but if it's all right with you, I'd like to stay here with Jamie."

"That works for me if that works for you. Are you sure that you are okay with that?" Peter asked insincerely.

Tina knew that was his plan all along. As disappointing as it was to know that she would be sitting alone at home with her baby once again, avoiding another one of his violent rages was worth it, so she said, "Yes, I want you to go and have fun for the both of us. There is no point in both of us having to stay home when one of us is enough to do the job of babysitting."

Peter was pleased to get his way but was pondering her statement, trying to determine if she was being sarcastic.

Tina decided to change the subject before he could respond. "I almost forgot to mention that my life insurance policy was delivered today."

"Okay, that's good. Where is it?" Peter asked.

"You want to see it?"

"Sure," he said nonchalantly.

She retrieved the policy from the end table beside her, handed it to Peter, and said, "Here it is."

After being satisfied with his inspection of the policy, he placed it inside of his backpack, which was then zipped closed and placed beside his motorcycle helmet.

"What are you planning on doing with it?" Tina asked.

"What?" he asked.

"The life insurance policy – why did you put it in your backpack?"

"I'm taking it to my mother's house for safekeeping."

"Why? What's wrong with keeping it here?"

"Because it's stupid to keep a life insurance policy here, that's why," he said with a raised voice.

"Why is that stupid?" Her suspicions were aroused.

"Because if something were to happen, the policy needs to be where someone knows where it is. I mean what if this place burned down or something? The policy would burn up too. Geez, do I have to do all the thinking for us?"

Despite his condescending insults, Tina thought that was a reasonable explanation. "Where is *your* policy?"

"It's at my mom's house, for safekeeping," he answered in an increasingly belligerent tone. "She has a fireproof safe."

She could tell that it was risky to continue this discussion, but she was afraid that if she didn't ask to see his policy now, it would be even more difficult to address the subject later. "Oh, that's smart. Who is your life insurance with?"

"Farm Bureau."

Her suspicions were more aroused. "Do you mind bringing it home with you so that I can look at it?"

"What the fuck! You don't trust me?" he said loud enough that she was concerned the neighbors could hear through the apartment's thin walls.

"Of course, I trust you; I just want to see it, like you saw mine." Her voice was elevated also, despite her trying to avoid a confrontational tone.

Peter stood and paced the floor, obviously agitated. "I saw yours because it's right here. You must not trust me! One minute you are bitchin' about my not making enough money, and the next thing you know, you don't trust me."

"What? I never complained that you don't make enough money. Where did that come from?"

"Just a few minutes ago, you said that $30 isn't enough to buy groceries. I work a full-time job and go to school full time so that I can get a better paying job when I graduate."

Tina realized that he was trying to change the subject, so she redirected the conversation. "It's not a matter of trust, I just want to give my father a copy of the policy number and beneficiary page for safekeeping, you know, in case your mother's home burns down."

"I told you; she has a fireproof safe!"

Tina's posture stiffened, her nostrils flared, and her eyes widened, but before she could reply, Peter said in a calmer tone, "Okay, okay. I will bring you a copy of my policy. Just stop bitchin'."

Satisfied that her goals were accomplished while avoiding another of his violent episodes, she quietly finished her meal.

Halloween was on a Friday that year. Tina dressed Jamie in a Batman costume. She decorated her front door and windows with cobwebs and spiders. She turned off the lights in their apartment and then turned on a strobe light for a ghoulish effect. She lit tiny candles in other parts of the apartment such as the bathroom and kitchen, making sure all were well out of Jamie's reach.

She filled a plastic jack-o-lantern with candy to provide trick or treaters who might knock on her door, but there were few children living in her apartment complex. Oxford is a college town, and almost all her neighbors were college students. Peter had been gone for hours, supposedly to the frat party, when she blew out the candles, turned off the strobe lights and fog maker, locked the doors, and went upstairs with Jamie to sleep.

Tina woke to the sound of sirens and the smell of foul smoke. The streetlight outside of her bedroom window illuminated her room enough for her to see a thick gray cloud just above her head. She turned her head toward her bedroom door which was closed. Through the cracks on the side, top, and bottom of the door she could see smoke billowing through an orange flickering light. She could hear the loud popping sound of fire burning. Her instinct was to jump up and rush to save Jamie, but she had been taught well by her father to keep her head in an emergency, and what to do in this situation. She rolled out of bed, pulling her blanket with her. She crawled to Jamie's baby bed and put the blanket over her nose and mouth before standing. She lifted Jamie from the bed and carried him to the only window in the tiny bedroom, leaning forward as she walked to keep her head below the cloud of smoke that had already filled the top half of the room. She raised the bedroom window, wrapped Jamie with the blanket, and then leaped, feet first, from her second-floor window to the pavement below. She knew to bend her knees and roll upon contact with the ground so that her legs would reduce the impact of her fall before her upper arm and shoulder took the balance of the impact. She felt a sharp pain in her ankle, but she had protected her head, and most importantly, Jamie.

She quickly began unwrapping Jamie to confirm that he was all right. The first responder to her was a fireman. She had not panicked until now. "Is my baby all right? Is he okay?" she screamed at the fireman, as tears filled her eyes for the first time.

The fireman inspected Jamie, who had just begun to cry, not from an injury, but from being disturbed from his sleep. "Your baby appears to be unharmed, but I want you both taken to the hospital to be checked out. Are you hurt?"

"My ankle hurts, but that's about all. I think that I am okay."

By the time she was placed in the ambulance, the entire

apartment building was engulfed in flames. She witnessed flames spewing out of her bedroom window as if from a flamethrower, the window from which she had jumped.

Virtually every college student had a cell phone. So, word of the fire spread quickly, and so were the rumors. Tina overheard someone say that some people had died. Peter had heard the same and checked his cell phone to see a couple of missed calls from numbers that he didn't recognize. One was from the fireman who first arrived to help Tina. The fireman informed Peter that Tina and Jamie were taken to the hospital.

"Oh my God, are you alright?" He asked in a melodramatic tone upon seeing Tina in the hospital emergency room.

"Yea, I'm fine, just a torn ligament in my ankle, that's all. Jamie had no apparent injuries at all, but they want to keep us overnight for observation," Tina replied calmly.

"That is great news, but I bet you were terrified," Peter said, as he gently rubbed her leg just above her ankle.

"It was frightening, and have you seen the apartment building? I am sure that we lost everything that we own."

With unusual compassion, Peter said, "The important thing is that you and Jamie are unharmed. The things we can replace. We didn't have much, to begin with."

Tina's father, Paul, and her sister, Liz, arrived at the hospital the following morning in time to take her and Jamie to her apartment to retrieve her car. Peter followed behind on his motorcycle. He had spent the night in the hospital room with her and Jamie. Paul was the father of five children. As such, he had become a proficient planner, prepared for all sorts of contingencies. He brought with him a spare set of keys to her car which was unharmed by the fire.

"I am so glad you thought of this, Dad. My keys were in my purse which was in the apartment. What would I do without you?" Tina said with all sincerity.

"That's what I'm here for, baby. Now, what are your plans? Do y'all have a place to stay right away?" Paul said, looking at Peter for an answer.

"We don't have a plan. This happened so suddenly," Peter replied.

"Since you are still in school and have a job, do you have a place to stay here in Oxford, while I take Tina and Jamie home with me to Pascagoula until y'all can sort out where you will live next?"

"Yeah, I have some buddies that will let me crash for a little while."

"That settles it then. Liz, you drive Tina and Jamie in her car to my house in Pascagoula. I will follow you," Paul said to Liz.

"Give me just a few minutes to go through Tina's car to get anything that belongs to me before you drive away," said Peter.

"While he is doing that, I am going to walk through this debris to see if there is anything salvageable," Paul said, as he turned his attention to the smoldering apartment building.

"Be careful, Dad, that wood is still hot. Smoke is still rising," said Liz.

Tina and Liz watched their dad closely, as he stepped into the charred remains of her apartment building. He used his foot to stir the debris, looking to see if there was anything worth saving.

Investigators saw Paul step past the police tape, and they walked toward him.

"Come on, Dad. There is nothing worth taking a chance on getting hurt or arrested, and you are going to smell like smoke," Liz said.

Paul agreed that it was a waste of time searching through

the debris.

"Sir don't disturb this area," said the police officer.

"Yes sir, I'm sorry. This is my daughter and her child. They lived here and I was looking to see if any of their belongings were salvageable," Paul responded respectfully to the officer.

"I understand, but this is a crime scene," said the officer.

"What happened? Was this set deliberately?" asked Tina anxiously. She had assumed the fire started from a candle that hadn't been extinguished properly.

Peter approached to listen carefully to the officer's response.

"We don't know yet, but we are investigating it as if it were until we find out differently. There were six people who died here last night, and their families deserve answers. Since you lived here, I have questions for you."

"Okay," Tina replied.

The officer questioned Tina and Peter about how long they had lived there, and what they were doing prior to and during the fire. Tina told her story and Peter said that he had been at a frat party.

Paul treated the group to lunch at Proud Larry's before driving to Pascagoula. As planned, Liz drove Tina's car while Paul followed behind in his car. Tina opened her prescription bottle of pain medicine and popped a pill in her mouth and washed it down with a swig from her water bottle.

"How does your ankle feel?" Liz asked Tina.

"It hurts like hell."

"I'm sorry that your apartment burned, and that you hurt your ankle, but I am so thankful that you and Jamie weren't seriously hurt or killed."

"Yes, I am thankful also."

"Hmmm, that's strange," Liz said as she steered the car to exit Highway 98 and merge onto Highway 63, southbound toward Pascagoula.

"What's strange?"

"Your brakes didn't feel as though they were working very well when I made that last turn," Liz answered.

"What do you mean?"

"I had to press the brake harder than before to slow the car down."

"They are fine, dad checked them just recently. You know how he is. You aren't accustomed to driving my car, that's all."

"You're probably right. By the way, I have some extra clothes that you can have if you want."

"Yes, I want them, sight unseen. Beggars can't be choosey."

"What do you think caused the fire?".

"I don't know. It was Halloween. Maybe someone left a candle burning or something. I can't imagine that someone would start it on purpose."

"It's so sad that all those people burned to death. Did you know any of them?"

"No, we didn't have much interaction with our neighbors. Peter was gone so much with his job and school and all, and I was like the only one in the apartment complex with a baby."

"Do you need anything?"

"I need you to hurry up and get to dad's house, I have to pee," Tina replied.

"I'm driving seventy-five miles an hour, ten miles over the speed limit. I'm not going any faster than that but will pull over at the next store that I see."

They were traveling south on Highway 63, which is straight and flat, allowing one to see what was ahead for many miles. There is only one signal light on Highway 63 between Highway 98 to the north and Interstate 10 to the south. Liz could see the signal light from several miles away. "Do you want me to stop at the store coming up?" she asked.

"No, keep going. I can wait."

A few minutes later, the light turned red. As she began to apply the brakes, she said, "It looks as if we are going to catch this light anyway, so tell me if you want me to stop— oh, no!" Liz interrupted herself.

"What is it?" asked Tina, alarmed by Liz's panicked tone of voice. Then she noticed Liz's right leg pumping the brake pedal, but nothing was happening.

"Oh, my God, the brakes are out! Call dad and ask him what to do!" Liz screamed.

Tina instructed her to "Keep calm and put the car in neutral. If we can get past this light, we can coast to a stop." She started searching through Liz's purse for her cell phone to call their father who was following them but had fallen behind a few miles.

They could see a line of cars crossing the highway on both sides; one line traveling east and the other traveling west, dissecting their southbound path.

"Oh my God, there are cars coming through the intersection! We are going to get there at the same time!" Liz warned.

Tina looked over her shoulder to see if Jamie was buckled into his carrier seat as snugly as possible.

Liz was about to panic, "What should I do?!"

Tina and Liz knew this highway well. It was well paved and stripped with wide shoulders. There was a drainage ditch in the otherwise wide barren median. There was nothing but grass between the shoulders for about fifty yards or so, then there was a thick wall of skinny scrub pine trees as far as one could see.

"You may have to run off the road… but do whatever it takes to keep from hitting something head-on," Tina said as she turned on the emergency blinkers.

Liz began blasting the car's horn repeatedly and swerved from one lane to the other hoping to draw the attention of the drivers crossing their path. With just seconds to go before reaching the intersection, both women realized there was nowhere to go to avoid crashing into another car other than veering off the highway, risking hitting a tree. The median was the safest way to exit the highway, for it was barren of trees. Thankfully, there wasn't a curb or other obstruction.

The car had slowed to about sixty miles an hour when they made the decision to exit the pavement. Although the median was covered in grass, it made for a bumpy ride before the car began to sway. Suddenly, before the girls had time to think, the car rolled over at least twice before coming to a stop, resting upside down.

Tina opened her eyes to a shattered windshield. There was no sound at all at first. The silence was deafening. Then she heard a hissing sound. Then she heard Jamie crying. She turned around and although upside down, he was still strapped into his car seat and appeared uninjured. She looked at Liz, who was just regaining consciousness. The airbags had been deployed. Suddenly the smell of smoke alerted Tina to the realization that the car's engine may be on fire. She sprang into action. Unbuckling her seatbelt, she managed to crawl from the mangled car through the window. By this time, others had rushed to their aid. Despite her swollen ankle, she sprang to her feet to open the door for Jamie, but the door wouldn't open.

Thankfully, one of the good Samaritans was a volunteer firefighter who lived in the area. He had a tool to pry the door open and rescued Jamie then Liz. Tina later regretted that she failed to get his name.

Another good samaritan who arrived was an off-duty nurse who told each of them to sit while she examined them. The fireman handed the girls their cell phones. Tina called her father, Paul, who had stopped for coffee and fallen behind.

The nurse checked Tina's pulse and asked her standard medical questions when she heard the sirens of the approaching police car. Paul arrived on the scene shortly after Tina finished reporting the accident to the deputies. He was visibly shaken but maintained his composure for the girls' sake.

The ambulances arrived before Tina could tell the whole story to Paul. He was confident they were not seriously injured so he watched the ambulances take his family away and decided to stay behind to see what he could learn from the deputies.

For the second time within twenty-four hours, Tina was in an ambulance on her way to a hospital. This time they were taken to Singing River Hospital in Pascagoula. They were scratched and bruised, but miraculously, they had no serious injuries.

They were still in the hospital emergency center's waiting room when Liza's phone buzzed. It was Paul, calling from the crash site. He spoke with her for a minute and then she handed the phone to Tina.

"Tina, are you sitting down?"

"No, I'm standing, why?"

"I want you to sit down. Where is Jamie?"

"He is here with me, in my arms. Why? What is the matter?"

"Hand Jamie to Liz, and tell me when you are sitting down," he said with firm authority.

"Dad, you are scaring me, what is it?"

"*Do it!*" he said more firmly.

She did as he instructed. "Ok, I am sitting down, now what do you have to tell me?"

"The Sherriff's investigation into your car accident revealed that your brake line was cut intentionally."

There was a pause for her to process his words, but once she realized the meaning of his message, Tina dropped the cell phone in her lap. She was in shock.

Hours later, they were all reunited at Paul's home. They had not fully recovered from the shock when Paul asked Tina, "Who would want to harm you?" He could not bring himself to say "kill" or "dead," and he suspected Peter right away, but he didn't want to be the first to suggest that. If Peter was innocent, their relationship would be forever damaged if he accused him of attempted murder.

"How can we be certain that someone does?" She asked.

"Your brake line was severed intentionally, and you were nearly killed in an apartment fire last night," I think that we are pretty sure that someone is out to get you. The question is who has a motive?"

Tina's heart sank. She knew the answer. The beneficiary of her life insurance policy has a motive. He had been so adamant about her getting a policy too. At first, she applied for a million-dollar policy based on Peter's recommendation, but the insurance company refused to sell her more than a quarter-million-dollar policy.

She wasn't ready to tell her father that she suspected Peter because she was afraid that her father might go into a rage and do something that could get him hurt or in trouble. She needed to be 100 percent certain before she accused Jamie's father of such a heinous crime.

Paul had never liked Peter from the beginning. "You aren't leaving this house or my side until we get to the bottom of who is trying to hurt you," he said.

Liz said to Tina, "You should tell Dad about the life insurance policy."

"What life insurance policy?" Paul asked.

With a quick glance at Liz, Tina answered her father, "I was going to wait until tomorrow or the next day to tell you so that you have time to calm down, but now that the cat is out of the bag, I suppose I should tell you…

Tina explained how Peter insisted they buy life insurance, making one another the beneficiary so if something happened to one of us, the survivor could afford to raise Jamie. Tina realized at that moment whoever was trying to kill her was also trying to kill Jamie!

Paul could not hide his suspicions any longer or his anger. He paced the floor, thinking of what to say next. He then turned to Tina and said, "Give Peter a call. Let him know that you made it home safely. Then tell him that you miss him already and want him to come here tomorrow to be with you and Jamie."

"Dad, what are you planning? Please don't do anything. Let the police handle this. I could not bear to have you go to prison on my account."

"I won't do anything that will land me in prison, but I want to see if he is willing to show his face around here. If he won't, then he is guilty as hell. If he shows, I plan to trap him into saying something incriminating. One thing is certain; you will cancel your life insurance policy as soon as possible."

Tina used Liz's cell phone to dial Peter's number. He didn't answer, but Tina left him a voice mail. "Hey honey, I just wanted you to know that we all made it to Dad's house safely, and I miss you. Please call me back on Liz's phone." She tried to sound as natural as possible but feared her voice betrayed her.

Paul called the officers investigating the apartment fire in Oxford first, and then he called the deputy that he spoke to at the crash site in Jackson County, where the car crashed. He shared his reasons for suspecting Peter of being the culprit in both cases. Everyone involved agreed not to let Peter know that he was a suspect until more evidence against him could be obtained.

Liz's cell phone rang. It was Peter. Liz handed the phone to Tina but held her head against the backside of the phone to hear the conversation. Paul leaned in to listen as well.

"Hi sweetheart, I'm glad y'all made it to your dad's house

safely. How is your ankle?" Peter acted as if everything was normal, but Tina detected caution in his voice. She thought he sounded guilty, but it was too early to show her cards.

"My ankle still hurts a little, but the pain medicine helps a lot. I really miss you. Please drive to Pascagoula to visit me for the day tomorrow." She sounded convincing, but she displayed an angry face to Liz and Paul.

"I miss you, too, but I can't drive my motorcycle down there. My tag is expired, and my brake light is out. You should bring Jamie with you to Oxford for the day tomorrow."

Liz shook her head from side to side, indicating her disapproval.

"I can't drive because I'm taking pain medicine. Maybe you can get one of your friends to bring you. Please!"

Tina's nature wasn't to plead, and she hadn't mentioned having trouble with her brakes, so this may have alerted Peter to her suspicions. "We will see. I will let you know tomorrow. Bye for now."

Peter didn't call the next day, which was Sunday, and Tina did not attempt to call him either. She was getting angrier by the hour and doubted she could fake being happy another time.

The following day was Monday. Tina called the insurance agent and instructed him to cancel the life insurance policy immediately.

"Sure, I will cancel, but you've already paid the premium for the month, so you still have coverage until the end of the month, plus an additional thirty-day grace period," he explained.

Paul was listening to the conversation and instructed Tina to change her beneficiary immediately.

"Yes, I can send a form to change your beneficiary immediately upon receiving a fax from you instructing me to do so, but I will need a wet signature on the form."

Tina followed the agent's instructions, and upon receiving the form, she had her signature notarized and mailed it to the agent in the overnight express mail. A day later, she received confirmation that her father was now the named beneficiary.

A short time later, the agent called. "Ms. Tina, I just wanted to inform you that I received a call from your previous beneficiary that he wanted to change the mailing address of your policy. I explained to him that the only person who can make any changes to the policy is the policy owner, you. However, I thought that you might want to know."

"Thank you, Mr. Thomas. I appreciate the information. By

the way, what address did he want to change it to?"

"We didn't get that far. Once I explained he couldn't make the change, he hung up on me."

Tina dialed Peter's number. "Hello?" he answered.

"Hi, Peter. I just got a phone call from my life insurance agent; he said that you wanted to change the mailing address. What is that all about?"

"I thought it best to change the address to my mother's address now that the apartment has burned," he replied with no hesitation.

"Oh, I see. Well, I think it's best to have my mail come to my daddy's house since I am here, and not at your mom's house, so I changed the address to this one. By the way, what is the name of the company that issued your life insurance policy?"

"Liberty Life, or something like that, I will have to look."

She noticed that he provided a different answer each time she asked. How could he not know the name of his life insurance company when it was so important to him in the first place?

"Please do and get me the policy number while you are at it," she said firmly.

"Okay, but why do you need it?"

"I want to know where to collect my money when something happens to you," she said with an angry tone.

"*When* something happens to me?" Peter asked.

"Yes, you son of a bitch, and I've changed my beneficiary to my father so you can stop trying to kill me!" Tina ended the call.

"Well so much for not letting him know that he is a suspect!" Liz said.

"I'm sorry, I just couldn't restrain myself. The thought that he was willing to kill Jamie also is too much for me to keep inside."

They didn't hear from Peter after that day. His cell phone had been disconnected, and his mother swore that she had no idea of his whereabouts. The FBI searched for him, and they couldn't find him anywhere, until two years later.

Chapter 7: Peter Found

Saturday, August 27, 2005

Singing River Hospital, Pascagoula

Tina pushed the button on the control which raised her hospital bed so that she could sit upright, in a better position to eat breakfast. Her appetite had improved, and she was hungry for the first time in days. The television was tuned to Biloxi's WLOX. The news of the day was Hurricane Katrina. The scenes were mostly of New Orleans, but an occasional clip of the Mississippi Coast would appear as the reporter reported: "Hurricane Katrina is officially a category FIVE, which is as bad as it gets folks. This is a serious storm, not to be taken lightly. For those of you unfamiliar with hurricanes, the most powerful rating for a hurricane is category Five."

Using the remote control, she changed to another channel, this one out of Mobile. On the television screen was the Mayor of New Orleans giving the most dramatic news conference from a public official; "This is the big one that we have always feared. As any New Orleans resident can tell you, this is a city that is below sea level. No hurricane has hit the Crescent City head-on in modern times, especially a Category five hurricane. As mayor of this great city, I am ordering all citizens to evacuate this city immediately. You must go because all law enforcement agencies will be evacuating as well. This will be a dangerous place to be if you choose to remain. I urge you not to stay."

The next image on the television showed the Gulf of Mexico nearly covered by Katrina's outstretched tentacles. Experts began making dire predictions and began to explain what might happen if New Orleans was to take the brunt of Category 5, the biggest and most powerful of all hurricanes.

"New Orleans is actually below sea level" one talking head explained. "The levies that surround New Orleans were designed to keep water out but should a storm surge push water over the levy, the water would be held in by those levies… New Orleans would in effect become a bowl full of water."

Another reporter said, "All one must do is look at a series of satellite photos taken over a period of decades to see that the land south of New Orleans has disappeared at a rapid rate. This is the same land that has protected New Orleans for all these years and made it such a great place to build a city. Now we not only have the biggest of hurricanes threatening a direct hit on the city, but the city is also more vulnerable than ever."

Tina changed the channel again. The reporters on this station were discussing what impact this hurricane might have on the Mississippi Gulf Coast. One said, "Everything immediately east of New Orleans could receive a huge storm surge, possibly producing a wall of water as high as thirty feet."

Tina pressed the call button.

Within a few minutes, a nurse entered her room and asked, 'How can I help, sweetie?"

"I am sorry to bother you about this, but is there anything else that I can watch on television other than weather reports? It's bad enough that I am going to ride out the storm in the hospital, but I need something to take my mind off what is going on outside that window." Tina pointed to her window.

"That's a tough request, honey. There is a VCR connected to your TV, and every now and then someone will bring a movie up here for patients who have been with us for a while. I will be back in a few and let you know what I find out."

A short time went by before the nurse returned. She had a VHS tape in her hand. "The only thing that I could find is this; a nurse recorded Dateline last night and brought it to work this morning to watch it. Do you want to watch it?"

"Sure, anything is better than watching the same weather reports over and over. Thank you for your efforts."

"You're welcome, I hope that you enjoy this." said the nurse.

"You are very thoughtful, what is your name?" asked Tina.

"My name is Janice. I will be your nurse for the next several days, as I've decided not to evacuate. I will be here with you until the storm has passed and it's safe for others to return."

"Thank you, Janice. I'm Tina."

"Yes, I know," said Janice with a smile as she inserted the VHS tape into the player. "It should switch over automatically, but I will wait for a minute to make sure that it comes on for you."

Within seconds, the picture and sound on the television changed to the introduction of the investigative news program, Dateline.

"There you go. I am going to leave you, but you can let me know if you need anything else," said Janice.

Tina was relieved to have something to watch on television other than reports of Hurricane Katrina. Why watch depressing news about an approaching storm when there was nothing, she could do about it. She couldn't evacuate. She had been admitted for having blood poisoning.

On the television, the investigative reporter told the story about a wealthy but elderly woman, eighty years or so, who had been conned into marriage by a much younger man in his twenties. Shortly afterward, the con man convinced his young girlfriend to murder the old lady so that they could live together on her money. The television screen is filled with mug shots of the young con artist. Tina nearly lost her breath. She recognized that guy on the television screen.

It was Peter!

She said to herself, "Oh my God, oh, my God," repeatedly as she scrambled to dial her father's telephone number. She was on the verge of hyperventilating and couldn't get the words out.

"What is it? Are you okay? If not, call the nurse and I am on my way up there," Paul told his daughter.

"Yes, please come, and bring Liz with you!"

Paul had been busy preparing his home for the coming storm. Plywood covered all his windows, and everything which could be picked up and blown threw the air by hurricane winds had already been put away. He put his cell phone in his pocket and called for Liz to get Jamie and meet him in the driveway. Liz followed his instructions and soon they were in the hospital room with Tina, watching the recorded program. She restarted the recording from the very beginning. Peter had grown a mustache, dyed his hair, and changed his name. In the end, his new girlfriend was awaiting trial for conspiracy to commit murder, but Peter had gotten away.

"Oh my God, Jamie's father is a murderer," said Tina.

"Darling, you knew that already. Have you forgotten that he set your apartment on fire and cut your brake line?" Paul asked.

"No, I haven't, but I made myself believe that it wasn't true, but now, it is so obvious that he had planned on killing me and Jamie!"

Liz ejected the tape and said, "Enough of this."

Chapter 8: Hunter

Sunday, August 28, 2005

Hunter covered the last of his windows with plywood when he received his instructions from his boss, Chief Harris. He put his cell phone away and made one last inspection of his one-story bungalow-style apartment to reassure himself that he had done all that he could to protect his belongings from the approaching storm. Then as he walked to his car, he looked across the street to see the choppy waves and white caps in the Pascagoula Bay, splashing against the seawall which was built to protect Beach Boulevard from such storms.

Looking back at his small apartment, he realized it was no match for a tidal wave. If Hurricane Katrina pushed a wall of water directly into this tiny home, he could lose all his worldly possessions. He wasn't concerned, though, because he hadn't had time to accumulate a lot of stuff since graduating from the Coast Guard Academy a few years ago.

His apartment was on the grounds of a former golf resort and hotel known as the Longfellow House, a beautifully restored anti-Bellum home, named for Henry Wadsworth Longfellow, who supposedly spent time there. Hunter admired the home and the numerous ancient mossy Oaks. The huge trees, with their twisted limbs stretching out far from their trunks, often touching the ground, had survived countless hurricanes. Knowing that these trees and the Longfellow House had survived all these years gave Hunter hope that his apartment could survive as well. But then he reasoned that his apartment was built in modern times, and they don't build them like they used to. He wasn't as concerned with the possible loss of his things as he was with the thought of having to find another place to live. Where else can a young man in his late twenties afford a place located on a golf course, with a view of the Gulf of Mexico, surrounded by the most beautiful trees in the world, and within walking distance to a fabulous restaurant, pool, clubhouse, and gymnasium? Nowhere that he could think of other than Pascagoula.

The traffic on Highway 90 to Mobile was thick and slow. The trip, which is normally a thirty-minute drive, took over two hours. Hunter gave his credentials to the guard who opened the gate allowing him to enter the Coast Guard's property. He parked his car and entered the building where he met with his counterpart.

On his return trip to Pascagoula, Hunter tightly gripped the steering wheel to keep the high winds from blowing his Ford F-150 into oncoming traffic. This was particularly important since all the other lanes directed traffic in the opposite direction, away from the Mississippi Gulf Coast and toward the city of Mobile.

The trailer in tow was filled with supplies meant for his crewmates. Despite the heavy load, the trailer swayed, causing Hunter grave concern.

He received a call, shortly after entering Mississippi, from his commanding officer, asking "Where the heck are you, Lieutenant? You should have been here by now. How much longer before you are here with those supplies?"

"It's hard to say, sir. Under normal circumstances, I would say that I could be there in about twenty minutes, but they have I-10 closed to one lane going toward Pascagoula, and the traffic ahead of me is moving at a snail's pace."

"You need to turn on your blues and do whatever you can to get here within an hour, because the *Yorktown* has been ordered to evacuate, with or without you."

Hunter activated the truck's blue emergency lights, and said, "Yes sir. I will get there as quickly as I can. What is the most recent report?"

"It's bad. The storm has intensified to category five and has changed course slightly to the east. It is projected to make landfall in a matter of hours, just east of New Orleans, maybe hit Bay St. Louis dead on. Hurry, son. You don't want to miss the boat."

Hunter steered his truck onto the shoulder of the interstate highway to pass the stalled traffic in the lane in front of him but could see within a short distance a highway patrol car with blue lights flashing, stopped on the shoulder, preventing him from proceeding. Hunter lowered his window to speak with, and to show his Coast Guard badge to the patrolman.

The patrolman spoke first, "You are going the wrong way, all westbound traffic from this point forward is halted."

"This is an emergency. I must get to the Coast Guard Station with these supplies."

That is a tough challenge that you have. All lanes from this point forward will have the traffic coming toward you and there are several disabled vehicles on the shoulder preventing you from getting very far. The bridge will be impossible for you to go against traffic. I suggest that you get off the interstate as quickly as you can and take another route. I wish that I could escort you, but I have to stay here to turn this traffic around. The only thing that I can do for you, is to halt this traffic long enough so that you can get past this point, but after that, you are on your own."

"I understand, officer."

"Good luck to you, son."

With the patrolman's help, Hunter maneuvered the truck and trailer past the patrolman's car and back onto the interstate shoulder. Just as the patrolman had said, Hunter quickly encountered a disabled car on the shoulder of the highway, preventing him from proceeding. He hopped out of the truck, holding his badge high as he stepped in front of the oncoming traffic. He instructed the driver of a car to remain put until he could drive around the disabled vehicle and return to the shoulder of the highway. He had to repeat this process three more times before he was able to exit the interstate. Each stop cost valuable time. Traveling Highway 90 to the city was much easier, but he was way behind schedule.

The Coast Guard Station in Pascagoula was located on Singing River Island, accessible only by a tall bridge. No one was manning the guardhouse at the base of the bridge as was the norm.

Hunter dialed his commanding officer's number. "Sir, I am at the gate, but the gate is locked and there is no one here to unlock it."

"You missed the boat, Lieutenant," came the response.

Hunter felt queasy. "What do I do now sir?"

"I don't know what to tell you, son."

"Well, I have this trailer full of supplies."

"Yes, we sure could have used those supplies."

"I'm sorry sir. I did my best to get there in time. Now, what are my orders?"

"Your orders are to do whatever you deem prudent. Good luck" said his CO before ending the call.

Hunter sat there for a minute, contemplating his next move. He turned on the radio to hear the emergency reports.

The governor was heard to say, "Everyone is hereby ordered to evacuate all Mississippi Gulf Coast counties. This is a *mandatory* evacuation. I repeat, *mandatory*. This includes all law enforcement and first responders, which means if you do not evacuate, you will be on your own to defend yourself. It is highly likely that you will be without power and water for several days. There will be a risk of infection and disease if you stay behind. This is not a storm to be taken lightly. There *will* be a storm surge associated with this storm, which will likely devastate everything within several blocks of the shoreline. This hurricane is expected to be more devastating than Camille. But, if for whatever reason you cannot evacuate and you must ride out the storm, I encourage you to go to the nearest county courthouse building or hospital. Those are typically the safest shelters during a hurricane."

Hunter contemplated evacuating. But to where? His family lived far away, in Virginia. Using the internet on his smartphone, Hunter checked the local radar map to see when and where Katrina was expected to make landfall. Then he checked the fuel level on his truck – a quarter of a tank. It had taken three-quarters of a tank to pull the heavy load from Mobile to Pascagoula. He reasoned that his priority should be to refuel, so he turned the truck around and headed back across the bridge to the first gas station in Pascagoula. It was closed. There were two other stations across the street, both also closed. Pascagoula was a virtual ghost town by now. Few cars were on the road, and all the businesses were boarded up and closed. He figured that the nearest place to purchase fuel is probably in Mobile. He could get there on a quarter of a tank if he weren't hauling such a heavy load, but he couldn't just abandon such an expensive cargo, so he reasoned that he should travel to the local hospital and ride the storm out there.

Singing River Hospital sits atop a rare hill in Pascagoula. It's a manmade hill, created by using the dirt from the duck-filled pond which serves as its landmark. Hunter drove past the pond to the main entrance to the hospital only to see that it had been boarded over with plywood. The sign directed him to the emergency entrance on the side of the hospital building. After parking his car across from the emergency entrance, Hunter removed his gun belt and holster, thinking it best to approach the hospital unarmed. There was a security guard and a policeman there to greet him. Hunter explained his circumstances to the pair.

The policeman introduced himself as Jay Hebert and explained that he was there in an unofficial capacity since all law enforcement officials had been ordered to evacuate. "I just couldn't leave this town, this hospital, unprotected without any law enforcement at all; not with all these patients in here, and the hospital staff too," said the police officer.

"Same here. I've been working with these fine people for years. There was no way that I wasn't going to stay behind and help these folks," said the security guard, who introduced himself as Gerome Broussard.

Hunter noticed that both men were at least double his age. Officer Hebert had a potbelly, and although Mr. Broussard was thin and appeared to be in good shape, had some gray in his otherwise black hair. Hebert was armed with a gun, holstered to his side, but Broussard was armed only with mace and handcuffs.

"How many other guards remained to protect the hospital?" he asked of Broussard.

"There are four more of us," was his answer.

"I see that you aren't carrying a firearm, are any of the other guards armed?"

"No sir, the hospital policy is no firearms inside."

"Officer Hebert has a firearm, are you going to tell him that he can't take his gun inside?"

"No sir, I ain't tellin' nobody with a gun that they can't do nothing," came his reply, smiling as he shook his head side to side.

"The reason that I ask, is that I have a firearm in my truck, and would feel a lot better wearing it if we are the only law in town protecting this hospital."

Officer Hebert spoke up, "Yes, by all means, get it. I want all the backup that I can get when the lights go out...it's going to be like the zombie apocalypse around here."

"Nobody's gonna stop you here," said Broussard.

"There's something else," Hunter said. "That trailer that I'm towing behind my truck – it is filled with valuable items which will be useful after the storm, generators, and such, but there is also a cache of weapons and ammunition. It's locked up good, but I need to store it in a safe place, out of sight."

"I know just the place," replied Broussard.

"You go with him and show him where to put the trailer, and I will stay here and guard the entrance," said Hebert.

Broussard followed Hunter to his truck. Hunter opened the doors and strapped on his gun belt, holster, and gun, slid in behind the steering wheel, and then said to Broussard who was already positioned in the passenger seat, "I have an extra firearm and holster that you can borrow until the storm passes."

"No thank you, I don't think that I should."

"Can you handle a firearm?"

"Oh, yes sir. I was a policeman at one time, but I don't want to lose my job; hospital rules, you know."

Hunter backed his trailer into the hospital parking garage so that one would have to move the truck to steal the trailer. He said to Broussard, "Let me show you something." Using his key to remove the lock on the trailer doors, he swung open one of the trailer doors and pointed to several handguns and shotguns that were mounted on the inside wall of the trailer. "Just in case you change your mind at some point, I wanted you to know where to find these. The ammo is in these boxes here," he said as he patted a stack of boxes. Hunter closed and locked the trailer door and said, "the key will be with me, of course."

Broussard led Hunter into the hospital through the staff's entrance from the parking garage. "Since you will be protecting this place, I need to show you around a bit," said Broussard. The emergency room was as active as ever, filled with patients awaiting medical attention. The main entrance was a different story. No one sat behind the help desk. The hospital florist and gift shop were closed, and the windows and doors were covered with plywood. The second floor was for cardiac patients and ICU. The third and fourth floors were for less critically ill patients.

In all, there were nearly 300 patients and about a hundred hospital staff that were there for the duration of the storm. Broussard introduced Hunter to the other four guards who were on duty. The first that he met was a small, overweight, female security guard, who was in her late forties. Her name was Shandra. She wasn't an inch over five feet tall. The next guard was also a female, but she was young and fit. In fact, she looked tough. Her name was Kelly. She was in her twenties and was obviously a bodybuilder. The third was a man who appeared to be older and frailer than Broussard, by name of Kent. Hunter was relieved to meet the last guard, Tony, who was in his early thirties and was buff. He would be the one you want watching your back in a fight. Broussard also introduced Hunter to key members of the hospital staff, such as the chief medical director and the chief nursing officer. He was introduced to a few of the doctors and several nurses, including Janice, who worked on the fourth floor. No one commented on the fact that he wore a firearm on his hip.

"This is Lieutenant Steele, who has volunteered to serve as a temporary security officer," Broussard said to the nurses gathered around their station on the fourth floor.

"Please, just call me Hunter," he said to the ladies behind the station.

One by one they introduced themselves, Janice included. "We are pleased to have you with us, but hopefully the circumstances won't be too uncomfortable for you," she said. Janice had been a nurse at Singing River Hospital for twenty-five years. She was in her early fifties but looked as though she was at least ten years younger than her actual age. She had short blond hair, big blue eyes and a smile that is contagious.

After the guided tour, Hunter and Broussard returned to the emergency room where Officer Hebert had remained. Everyone's attention was focused on the television. New Orleans Mayor Nagin's head and shoulders filled the screen as he spoke in the direst tone, "This is the one that we've always feared in New Orleans, if you can get out, get out now."

Hunter walked outside to see what changes had taken place in the local weather. A gust of wind nearly knocked him over. Trees bent under the pressure of high winds. A stop sign could be seen in the distance swiveling at such a high speed, that Hunter expected it to take flight at any second. The sky had filled with ominous clouds. "It won't be long now," said Broussard who had followed him outside.

Before Hunter could reply, Kent's voice was heard coming from Broussard's walkie-talkie, "Boss-man, do you mind if I take a little nap in case it turns into a long night?"

"Yes, that is a good idea. Ask Kelly to do the same. We need to work in shifts for the duration," replied Broussard.

"That reminds me, I need to get my Southern Link phone from the trailer so that I can check in from time to time with the crew on the Yorktown. That's the name of my ship, Yorktown," said Hunter.

"You do what you need to do, but I think ole Kent has a good idea for you and Officer Hebert too."

"Yeah, what's that?"

"I think, that since you and Officer Hebert are the only two in this entire hospital with a gun, y'all should take turns sleeping so that we have one of you rested and alert at all times."

"That sounds like a good idea to me too," said Officer Hebert who had joined them without notice until now.

Hunter and Hebert agreed on a schedule in which at no time would both be asleep at the same time. The hospital provided them with an unoccupied room on the fourth floor for resting. Hebert went to bed right away, agreeing to wake up at one in the morning so that Hunter would not have to stay up past one a.m.

Hunter's alarm on his cell phone woke him at seven the following morning. He used the bed's controller to raise his bed so that he could sit upright. He turned the television to the news of the storm. Hurricane Katrina had made landfall just east of New Orleans. The big news of the hour was that a levee in New Orleans had been breached.

There was a knock on the door followed by a familiar woman's voice, "Hello, are you awake?"

"Yes, come in."

Janice opened the door and entered. "I would not have bothered you if I had not heard your alarm go off and the television come on. Can I get anything for you? Coffee? Breakfast?"

Hunter replied, "That is very thoughtful of you. I am

hungry, but I don't want to impose."

"You aren't imposing. I asked you if you wanted something. Besides, you are an unpaid volunteer, here to protect us; the least the hospital can do is to feed you. Now, what would you like?'

After taking Hunter's order, Janice tapped on the door to the hospital room across the hall and said, "Hello, are you awake yet?"

Janice could hear the patient's voice through the door, "Yes, I am."

Janice entered the room to see Tina with her cell phone in her ear.

Tina asked, "Please hold on for a minute, my nurse just entered the room."

"How are you feeling this morning, dear?" Janice asked.

"Much better, I think. Well, it comes and goes. One minute I feel fine, and a few minutes later I feel as if I am dying." Tina replied.

"Do you have an appetite?" Janice asked as she checked Tina's blood pressure and other vital signs.

Tina replied, "No, not really." Then she put the phone to her ear and said, "I talked to Dad a few minutes ago, and he said that his whole yard is covered with water, and he is worried that it may come into his house."

"Well, I really think that you should try to eat something, so I am going to bring you some breakfast and I want you to try to eat as much as you can," Janice instructed.

"Yes, ma'am, I will try," replied Tina, and then she continued talking on her cell phone. "Well, you know Dad. He wasn't going to evacuate with me in the hospital. I feel bad that he is riding out the storm on my account."

The howling wind and rain beat hard against the hospital windows. Those on the upper floors were not protected with plywood. Tina and Hunter could hear the loud cracks of thunder.

Janice returned to Hunter's room with his breakfast. She noticed that Hunter did not have a ring on any of his fingers, and asked "Do you mind if I ask you a personal question?"

"No. Ask away." Hunter replied.

"I don't see a ring on your finger."

Hunter thought at first that Janice, who was nearly twice his age, was asking for her benefit. "No. No wife or girlfriend.

Why do you ask?"

"Because there is this really sweet and attractive girl in the room across the hall who is about your age. Maybe you should check in on her when you have a chance."

"What's wrong with her? I mean, she is in the hospital. Is she contagious?"

Janice laughed, "No, she wouldn't be on this floor if she were contagious, and I wouldn't suggest that you check in on her if she were. I can't say what she is in here for; you know privacy laws and all, but I can tell you that she is expected to have a full recovery. You should check in on her. She is worried about her father. He didn't evacuate because he didn't want to leave town with her in the hospital."

Hunter's curiosity couldn't keep him from investigating the girl across the hall, so after finishing his breakfast, he showered, dressed, walked across the hall, and knocked on Tina's door.

"Come in," she said without knowing who was knocking.

Hunter entered the room. "Hi, I hope that I am not disturbing you, but Nurse Janice suggested that I check in on you."

Tina was embarrassed because she hadn't had makeup on in

days and her hair was matted from being bedridden, and this attractive young man was seeing her at her worst. She pulled her pillow to her head to hide her hair as best as she could, and replied with a red face, "No, you aren't disturbing me, but who are you?"

She saw his badge and thought he might be there to ask questions about Peter, who is still a fugitive at large. As embarrassed by her appearance as she was, she was pleased to see Hunter.

"I suppose that you can say that I am with hospital security, of sorts, but I am also in the Coast Guard. My name is Hunter Steele. I understand that your father didn't evacuate." He held out his hand to shake hers.

He couldn't help but notice her bright smile as she replied, "I'm Tina Collins. It's nice to meet you, and yea, that's right. My father is stubborn. He decided to ride out the storm in his home. He didn't want to leave me alone in town in case I needed him."

"He should come here, to the hospital. Can you call him?"

"Yes, I just talked to him. His entire yard is flooded, so he is afraid to leave the house. He's determined to protect his stuff from looters anyway."

"What is the address where he lives? I will try to check on him if I can."

"That would be great. Give me something to write on, and I will write it down for you."

He handed her a pen and note pad which were on the bedside table and said, "write down his phone number also, in case I need to call him."

"Ok," she said.

"...and yours too," he said.

She smiled and wrote her cell phone number on the paper below her father's address and number, and then drew a happy face.

"So, what are you in for?" Hunter said with a smile, as he took the paper from her.

"Ha, I feel as though I've been in jail. I have blood poisoning, and I am *so* ready to get out of this hospital."

"Is there anything that I can bring you?"

"How about a ladder so that I can escape from this room?"

"Ok, I will see what I can do, after I check on your dad."

"Thank you so much. If you can get him to come here, I would be *so* grateful."

"I will see what I can do but no promises."

The Longfellow House, Pascagoula, MS

Chapter 9: Hurricane Katrina

Hunter found Officer Hebert in the emergency room staring at the news report on the television. "How was it last night? Anything exciting happen?"

"No, all was quiet on the western front, but the lights haven't gone out yet. When they do...wild, wild, west," replied Hebert.

"I would like to check on a patient's father who didn't evacuate. If you and the rest of the team can live without me for an hour or so."

"I think we can survive that long without you. Just be home before dark. That's when the zombies come out."

Hunter didn't like leaving the trailer behind where someone could hook up to it and tow it away, but he calculated the odds of someone taking it within the short time he would be away and decided it was worth the risk. The wind was fierce, lifting his wiper blades off his windshield. The rain appeared to be blowing parallel to the ground. The truck's GPS directed him to the house. He was pleasantly surprised that it still worked. The road in front of Paul's house was submerged under a foot of water. Hunter thought it best to leave the truck's engine running as he waded through the water to Paul's door.

Hunter knocked hard and yelled loudly, "Coast Guard! Looking for Paul Collins. Please open up!"

Paul opened the door and with surprise said, "Who called the Coast Guard for me? Here, come inside out of the blowing rain."

"Your daughter, Tina, asked me to check in on you. She is in the hospital, as you know, and I have been quartered there for the time being."

"That is very nice of you, but I am all right."

"Sir, with all due respect, your home is on the verge of flooding. You're more than welcome to ride out the rest of the storm at the hospital."

Paul rubbed his balding head as if it would help him to think. "I don't think the water is going to get much higher. I stayed here throughout Hurricane Camille and never got any water in this house, so I think that I will stay. Tell Tina not to worry about me."

After a brief pause, Hunter responded, "Ok, but would you at least write my number down and call me if the water rises enough to enter your house?"

Paul agreed, and Hunter returned to the hospital. Along the

way, Hunter noticed a man standing on the front porch of his house. Hunter stopped and asked the man if he would like to ride out the storm at the hospital. The man accepted his offer and climbed into the passenger seat of the truck, extended his hand to shake Hunter's, and introduced himself, "Wallace Krebs. It's nice to meet you."

Hunter noticed the man's boat and trailer parked in the man's yard and said, "That's a nice bass boat. Do you fish often?"

"Yep, as often as I can. I retired so I have more time now."

"I have a favor to ask of you, Mr. Krebs," Hunter said looking the old man in the eye.

"What is it?"

"If push comes to shove, and I need a boat to rescue somebody, may I borrow your boat? I can guarantee that if anything happens to it, the Coast Guard will replace it."

"Sure, you can. I could use a new boat. Let me go get the key."

"If you don't mind, I would like to tow it to the hospital with us; put it in the parking garage out of the weather, that way I can get to it better if we need it. It will be safer there anyway."

Mr. Krebs reached for the door handle. "I'm in favor of that idea. Give me a minute."

Hunter towed the boat and trailer to the hospital parking garage and parked it next to the Coast Guard's supply trailer. He parked the truck sideways, blocking both trailers from potential thieves.

Hunter returned to Tina's room to give her the report. He noticed that she had showered, groomed her hair, and her face had more color, thanks to make-up.

"Oh my God, he is so stubborn," Tina said. "There is no reason for him to stay home when he could have been here. He drives me crazy. I am calling him now," she said as she dialed his number.

Hunter said, "Ok, I'll give you privacy to talk," and he turned to leave.

"No, wait. You can stay – please stay," she said as she put her phone down.

"Are you sure?" he asked.

"Yes, I would like for you to stay, if you don't have somewhere else to be."

"Ok. I will stay." He sat in the chair next to her hospital bed.

They talked for hours, oblivious to the storm that was blowing against the glass window. She told Hunter the whole story about her experiences with her ex-boyfriend, Jamie's father. They watched the recording of Dateline together.

Janice was happy to see that they were getting acquainted when she stopped in to check on Tina.

Meanwhile, at Paul's house, the water kept getting higher until it had begun to flood his home. By the time Tina called to check on him, he was in a chair on top of his dining room table. Water was a foot deep throughout his one-story home. Then the entire city lost electrical power. The television went off in Tina's room, but within seconds the hospital's generators restored power and the television was on again. But Paul was in the dark. Although the sun hadn't completely set, his windows were covered with plywood preventing sunlight from entering his house. For the moment, his only light was from his cell phone, but he assured Tina that he had candles and battery-operated lights, "so don't worry about me."

"It's time for me to convince your dad to abandon his house and come here to the hospital," said Hunter.

"Yes, it is, but it won't be easy. He is determined that he is going to stay there and protect his home from looters. As if his tools are *so* valuable."

"So, that's the *real* reason that he won't evacuate! I will assure him that I will make patrols to keep his house safe."

The entire hospital began to shake and rumble at that moment. It suddenly sounded as if a freight train was about to drive through the hospital, and before either of them could respond, the roof and ceiling above Tina's top-floor room were ripped completely off. Glass and debris started flying. Instinctively, Hunter laid his body across Tina's to protect her from falling debris. As suddenly as it started, the sound was gone, but Hunter could feel rainwater striking his back. More pleasantly, he felt Tina's body next to his for the first time. He liked it, and so did she. The joy lasted only seconds because his emergency training taught him to think quickly and act quicker. He quickly got onto his feet and looked around the room to survey the situation. The glass window was gone. The ceiling above their heads was missing.

The door flung open. It was Janice. She rushed to Tina's bedside, "Are you hurt?" she asked Tina.

"No, I'm fine. Not a scratch on me, thanks to Hunter."

"Are you hurt?" she asked while looking at Hunter.

"No, not hurt. We need to get her out of here to safety."

Janice agreed, and the two of them moved Tina, bed and all, to the elevator at the end of the hall. There were others on the top floor which needed to be moved for the same reason. They were all taken to the second floor. There were more patients than available rooms, so Tina's bed was parked in the hall, as were others.

When the commotion was over, the realization of what just happened sank in, and Tina said, "Oh my God, I can't believe that just happened! A tornado ripped the roof off the hospital right over our heads!"

"That was wild," said Hunter.

They became aware that they were holding hands at that moment.

"I hope that tornado didn't hit my dad's house. I need to call him. Where is my cell phone?"

"I have his number on my cell phone. I will call him." Hunter reluctantly let go of her hand to make the call.

Tina regretted that he was no longer holding her hand also but was relieved to know that he was calling her father.

"No answer, but don't worry. I will go get him now."

Her heart monitor revealed her excitement when Hunter kissed Tina on the cheek before he left.

The sign on the elevator instructed him to use the stairs except in an emergency. Kelly, a hospital security staff member, was guarding the first-floor entrance to the stairs. Hunter quickly understood why she was concerned that unauthorized people might attempt to go upstairs. There were a lot more people on the first floor of the hospital than before. Apparently, the rising waters and loss of power throughout the town were responsible for the increased number of refugees. Hunter asked Kelly, "Is everything under control down here?"

"It is for now, but there are some scary characters here that weren't here before. They are making a lot of noise and starting to get unruly."

Things weren't going well at Paul's house. The water had risen to the top of his dining room table. He could feel the table being lifted by the water, despite his entire weight holding it down. If the water were to rise another inch or so, the tabletop would be covered and his candles, lanterns, and lunch boxes would float away. It was time for him to make a move. He made the decision to flee to the attic, but first, he would call his children so that they would know where to tell the authorities to search if they couldn't find him later. Tina's phone was lost in the melee that ensued when the hospital roof was ripped off. She didn't answer, so he called his other daughter, Liz.

"Hey honey, I don't want you to worry, but I may not get another chance to call anyone. The power is out everywhere, and the water is at least four feet deep in my house. I am relocating to the attic, but I'm not sure how much longer I will have cell phone service. Try to get word to the other children."

Paul stepped off into the dark water. It was a creepy feeling. Other than the little bit of light that his candles, lanterns, and cell phone emitted, it was pitch black. The sound of the storm was deafening. His entire house shook violently. He didn't know if he was surrounded by snakes or who knows what, but he knew that he had to make it to the attic to survive. A lot of things were floating in the water – furniture, small appliances, and other things he could only imagine. The pulldown staircase was in the hall on the far side of the house. As he sloshed his way through the rising water, he dropped most of the things that he was carrying. By the time he had made it to the pull-down staircase, he had just his cell phone in one hand and a small ice chest in the other. To pull down the attic staircase, he had to have a free hand. He could either lose his cell phone or allow his ice chest to float for a few minutes and pray that it didn't sink or float away. Fortunately, neither happened, and he would learn to appreciate having the sandwiches, crackers, and water in that ice chest.

Paul anticipated that he might have to retreat to the attic during the storm. Waiting for him was a lawn chair, battery-operated lanterns and flashlights, a radio, blankets, pillows, a first aid kit, and an ax; just in case. Once situated in the attic, Paul noticed that he had a missed call from an unknown number. He hadn't saved Hunter's number on his phone.

Hunter answered Paul's call, "Hello Mr. Collins. Are you alright?"

"I am fine and dandy. How is Tina?"

"She feels much better, but an apparent tornado ripped a portion of the hospital's roof off. Rain is pouring in on the top floor. Fortunately, there were no injuries as a result. She has been moved to another floor. Have you lost power to your home?"

"Yes, I did; a few hours ago."

"We have power at the hospital, so I am on my way to get you – no arguments – I promised your daughter."

"No, don't come. You won't be able to get to me. My house is completely flooded, and I'm in the attic now. I have food and water, blankets, and a flashlight, so I will be fine right where I am until the water recedes. Stay there and take care of my daughter."

"No can do. I made a promise to your daughter, but I'm glad you told me that. I will bring a boat to get you."

"I have an ax. I can chop my way through the roof. Be very

careful, the wind is blowing very hard, and the water is choppy. I don't want you getting hurt on my account."

"Keep your cell phone handy. I will text you when I am ten minutes away."

Hunter spotted Hebert and Broussard standing a few feet apart from one another, each eyeing the crowd suspiciously.

"We're glad to see that you. Zombies are here." Hebert said.

"Yeah, that's right. How is everyone upstairs? Do they have that roof thing under control?" asked Broussard.

"It's a real mess. Water is still pouring in from the rain, but they've moved all the patients to the lower floors. All the rooms are occupied so they have patients in beds lining both sides of the halls on every floor."

"I would have sent some of my people up there to help, but I need as many eyes on this crowd as possible. Looks to me as if there is some drinking going on among some of these folks. Maybe more than drinkin' if ya know what I mean." Broussard replied.

"Who's drinking? I will put a stop to that." Hunter said, placing his hand on his holstered pistol, just to reassure himself that it was still there.

Hebert held his hand up, giving the hand sign for *stop*, and said, "No, don't say anything. They are still trying to hide it for the moment. Confronting them will just aggravate the situation. Besides, drinking is the least of our worries. It's the crackheads that we must worry about."

Hunter looked at his watch and knew that time may be of the essence to rescue Paul but knew these men would be more comfortable knowing that they had one more armed guard in the event the crowd became hostile. He reached into his pocket and then handed a key to Broussard. "Mr. Broussard, you remember what I showed you in the back of my trailer?"

"Yes, I do," he replied.

"I want you to hold this key for me just in case you need anything from the trailer. I have somewhere that I must go for a little while but will return as soon as I can."

"Where are you going in this weather? There is a hurricane blowing out there!" Broussard responded with a hand waving toward the exit door.

"I will be all right, don't worry. It's my job to rescue people during storms. I could use your help for a few minutes. Will you come with me to the trailer?"

Broussard agreed and the two men made their way to the

parking garage where, they rifled through the trailer to get several life vests, and other critical gear that he would need in a rescue attempt.

Hunter pulled Mr. Krebs's bass boat as far as his truck could go before the water was too deep. He launched the boat into the water and tied the boat's line to a utility pole, so that it would not float away while he moved the truck to higher ground. The metal boat rocked violently in the choppy water and hurricane-force winds. The water was rushing in from the gulf at such a furious rate entire homes appeared to be surrounded by a raging river. Hunter had been involved in many rescue missions in the Gulf of Mexico, but none had as much floating debris as what he saw here. There was evidence in the water that entire homes had been washed off their foundations. This gave Hunter a sense of urgency to reach Paul.

Hunter was very familiar with the city of Pascagoula but having all the streets hidden from view made it difficult to ascertain his location. The blowing wind and rain made it more difficult. All of Pascagoula between him and the Gulf of Mexico was now submerged. Only the rooftops remained above water. His portable GPS wasn't working, so he had to find his way based on memory. The sound of wind swooshing through the trees, booming lighting, the occasional tree snapping, rushing water, and debris smashing against the small metal boat challenged his senses, making navigating that much more difficult. There were several occasions when he thought the boat might capsize. Despite the challenges, he was certain that he had located the street where Paul lived. The rooftops protruding above the water were encouraging. There were thousands of homes that had been completely washed off their slabs by this time. Hunter counted the homes on the south side of the street, "one, two, there it is," he said to himself. There was no one on the roof. Hunter tried to text Paul, but they had lost cell service, so he blasted a bullhorn to alert him that he had arrived. Suddenly a beam of light appeared from a small hole on the north side of the roof. Paul had chopped a hole large enough for observation but wisely decided to remain in the attic.

Paul chopped into the roof with his ax, enlarging the hole. Once the hole was large enough for Paul's arm to fit through, he extended his arm and grabbed hold of the line that Hunter tossed at him. Paul tied the line to a stud that braced the roof inside of his attic, then began chopping until the hole was big enough for him to crawl out onto the roof.

Hunter was bent over, almost lying in the boat to reduce his wind resistance. The roof itself served as a breaker for the water, but the wind whipped around the house as if it were coming from all directions. After numerous attempts, Hunter managed to get another line to Paul, who secured it to another rafter.

Paul reached his hand back through the hole and untied the lines before he climbed into the boat with Hunter. Paul tried to thank Hunter for coming to his rescue, but the howling wind made verbal communication nearly impossible. Hunter knew what he was trying to say.

Three hours passed since Hunter had left the hospital. He and Paul were elated to be under the protected cover of the hospital's parking garage when Hunter noticed that the overhead lights were out indicating the hospital had lost power. He parked his truck, leaving the boat and trailer hitched to the back. Retrieved his walkie-talkie and called for Broussard, who responded, "This is Broussard. Is this Lieutenant Steele?"

"Affirmative," Hunter replied.

"Where are you, man?" Broussard replied with an alarming sound.

"I am in the parking garage, where I parked the Coast Guard trailer. What is the situation?"

"Aw man, all hell has broken loose. The hospital lost power shortly after you left, and like Officer Hebert would say, the zombies are out. Man, I'm telling you, don't go anywhere on the first floor. It's a riot down there."

"Shit! Where are you? Are the patients in danger?"

"Not now. We are all on the second floor guarding all the stairwells, preventing the zombies from coming up."

"Do you still have the key to the trailer that I gave you?"
"Right here in my pocket."

"Did you remove anything from the trailer, as I suggested?" Hunter did not want to chance anyone overhearing the conversation and learning that there were firearms in his trailer.

"No, man. I can't do that. Hospital policy, but you can, being a trained and certified law enforcement officer and all."

"I need to get that key from you because I am about to deputize some civilians," Hunter replied.

"You best go through the staff entrance that I showed you, and you will encounter Shandra there and she can tell you how to get to me."

"Roger that," Hunter signed off and led Paul to the staff entrance from the second level of the parking garage. The door was locked this time, so Hunter knocked, hoping to get Shandra's attention without alerting anyone else to their whereabouts.

"Get away from that door! If you try to come in here, I will bust you in the mouth!" Shandra shouted, not knowing who was on the other side of the door.

Hunter didn't want to shout, so he held his badge so that she could see it through the narrow glass window which was part of the thick metal door. The door was opened.

"You better be glad you was you, I was fixin' to tase you," Shandra said with full confidence in her voice.

"I'm sure you would have, and glad you didn't this time,"

"I ain't taken no crap off no crackheads. Who is that with you?"

"This is the father of one of the patients. He was trapped in his home, so I brought him here for shelter."

"You may not have done him no favors. Do you know about those fools on the first floor? What they doing?"

"Broussard gave me a brief report. What exactly is going on down there?"

"In a word, drugs. Those fools are tearing up the place looking for drugs. It's just a matter of time before they try to force they way to the higher floors."

"I need you to do something important for me. You see that I have a gun?" He patted his sidearm.

"Yes, but you ain't got to threaten me to get me to do you

no favor," Shandra said sarcastically.

"No, I mean, I can guard this entrance, but I need you to go get a key for me from Broussard and hurry back. It's important."

"Ok, but if anyone tries to come in this door, I want you to shoot them right between the eyes. You can't kill zombies unless you kill 'em in the brain, you know." Shandra said before hurrying away.

Hunter looked at Paul. "Can you handle a gun?"

Paul laughed and replied sarcastically, "Are you joking? This *is* Mississippi. Everyone here knows how to shoot a gun."

"But can you shoot a man without hesitation if necessary to defend yourself or others, such as your daughter?"

"Give me a gun, and I will blow as many bastards away as I need to in order to protect my family, and I will sleep like a baby tonight," Paul said convincingly.

"I hope it doesn't come to that, and you need to promise that pulling the trigger is absolutely necessary because once a gun is fired, we could be overrun by a drug-crazed mob, half of which may have their own guns."

"You have my word. I am not looking for a fight, but if it comes down to shooting a bad guy to keep him away from my daughter or anyone else for that matter; I won't hesitate." Paul said convincingly.

"I hereby designate you a deputy in the United States Coast Guard," Hunter said.

"Deputy? In the Coast Guard? Is there even such a thing?" Paul asked.

"No, there isn't, but don't tell anyone else that I may have to deputize."

After Shandra returned with the key, Hunter made his way to the trailer, and with Paul's help, took as many weapons and as much ammo as they could carry to the entrance Shandra guarded. Hunter handed her a gun belt, complete with a loaded gun and extra ammunition, and said, "Look, I realize that it's against hospital rules for you to have a firearm, but you are wearing a uniform with a badge, and the bad guys won't be worried about rules if they turn their attention on us."

Shandra took the gun. "So long as this is our secret. If I never have to use this, I never had it."

"Agreed," Hunter said, as he shook her hand and continued his way to make the same proposal to Broussard, Tony, Kelly, and Kent. They all agreed to arm themselves, so the hospital now had eight armed guards protecting the patients, staff, and civilians who were all crowded on the second and third floors.

Hunter and Paul took turns checking on Tina. Her condition had worsened, possibly due to the reduced medical attention resulting from the power outage and subsequent turmoil in the hospital. Hunter put his hand on her forehead and detected a fever. He leaned forward and told her, "I will be right back."

She grabbed his arm, preventing him from walking away. Then she pulled him close. "I want to thank you for saving my father. I don't know how I can ever repay you."

He smiled and said, "I'm sure we can think of something; maybe you can start by going on a date with me when you are fully recovered."

She gave him a big smile. "I would have gone out with you anyway." She wondered how he could be interested in her, considering her momentary sickliness, but she was thrilled, nonetheless.

He kissed her once again, but this time it was a quick one on the lips, and he said, "I will be back in one minute." He found Janice tending to another patient farther down the hall. He apologized for interrupting her but asked if she could give Tina something for her fever.

"Of course, I will as soon as I finish what I am doing here.

I'm happy to see that the two of you have hit it off.".

Hunter heard a plea come over his walkie-talkie. It was Hebert, "I need some help here. The crowd is becoming more confident. I think they are planning something."

Broussard was heard responding, "Yeah, like what?"

"Like storming this stairwell and overtaking me with sheer numbers, if they overpower me and get my gun..."

"I'm on my way," Hunter replied.

The mob had managed to open the door to the stairwell by the time Hunter reached Hebert, who held them at bay by blinding them with his police issue flashlight and his assuring them that there is a small, well-armed, police force for them to deal with if they proceeded up the stairs. The crowd was getting louder and more belligerent by that moment. Voices from behind the leaders could be heard encouraging those in the front to charge the officers, "They ain't going to shoot, get them."

There was a tall, thin, and glassy-eyed young man who appeared to be in his late teens and stood in front of the others. He seemed to be the de facto leader.

Shandra's distinct voice was heard speaking loudly as she arrived from behind Hunter. "Y'all need to cut out yo foolishness. There ain't nothing up here for you. There ain't no drugs, no money, nothing up here for you but hurt and pain, so go back down there and finish tearing up the first floor of this hospital like a bunch of wild animals. Hey! I know you. I know your folks too. You best get on out of here before I make you sorry that you ever came up in this place where people care for sick people. Go on!"

To the surprise of all those who were there to witness this, the leader turned around and made his way through the crowd, and the rest of the mob followed him. Shandra then closed and locked the door behind them. Hunter was impressed with the moxie of that five-foot-nothing woman. She isn't scared of anyone.

The hospital maintenance crew was able to restore power to the hospital using their diesel-powered generators. The mob made no more attempts to enter the second floor and by sunrise, Hurricane Katrina had passed.

Chapter 10: Aftermath

Hunter opened the door at the end of the stairwell on the first floor which had been the protective barrier between civilization and barbarism the night before. To his surprise, it was quiet. There was no longer the sound of a chaotic mob or the sound of wind or rain. There were people scattered all over the floor. Most were sleeping, but some were sitting or lying without making a sound. The place was a filthy mess. There were empty bottles and trash strewn about. The gift shop's glass windows were broken, and the place was looted. Hunter stepped over people to make his way to the emergency room. He was disgusted that these people who had nowhere else to go, were so disrespectful as to destroy the very place which provided them with shelter from the storm.

The hospital staff, with the help of the security detail, cleared all the people who were not injured from the critical areas which were needed to reopen the emergency room for business. People had already begun to arrive with storm-related injuries. Convinced that the hospital staff had the situation under control, Hunter felt the need to explore the city to see if there were people in need of being rescued.

Norman Ruble was renowned for his love of parties. He woke up in a soaked bed. His first thought was that he had regressed to his childhood days, but soon learned otherwise. Coming to his senses, he realized his home had been flooded. The water level inside his home was up to the top edge of his bed's mattress. Wading through the water in his briefs, he drew the window curtains to see the water level on the other side of the window was two feet higher than the water inside his home. Realizing the water pressure could break the window sending glass shards into him at any moment, he quickly moved away from the window. The howling wind shook the entire house. He knew he had to do something, so he made his way to the front door of his home, which faced north. He managed to open the door without being swept away by the rush of water. He held onto the door sill until the water inside equalized in pressure with the water outside. Then he pulled himself outside the door, where the rushing water washed him off his feet. Sprawled horizontally "like an alligator," he traveled through obstacles such as signs, houses, bushes, and trees, until he reached the railroad tracks, which run parallel to the beach, and rises about four feet higher than the surrounding terrain. This unintentional dam slowed the surge enough for Norman to get to his feet.

Crossing the tracks, he entered the first building he came to, a laundromat. Once sheltered from the blowing wind and bruising rain, he realized the gravity of his circumstances. He looked around for something to nurse his cuts and wounds. Once dressed in strangers' abandoned clothes, he left the laundromat and noticed coffins from the funeral home across the street floating in the choppy waters. This encouraged him to return to the laundromat for shelter. Suddenly, a huge blast of wind shook the huge glass picture window so much that he began to worry that the window might shatter, sending glass toward him. He didn't want to go back into the weather, so he crawled into a front-loading washing machine for protection. Soon, others entered the building and followed his example.

Hiding in the washing machine seemed like a good idea at first, but through the glass door, he could see the water rising and rushing toward the large glass pane window. When the windows were shattered and water rushed through the laundromat with fury, Norman and the others who had sought refuge as he had begun to fear being trapped and drowning in the machines. Fortunately, the water never rose high enough to enter the machine where Norman had found refuge. He rode out the entire storm protected by an industrial washing machine.

Hunter first saw Norman walking through a debris field, dressed in mismatched clothes that didn't fit his slender frame. Norman told Hunter about the others in the laundromat. The next few hours were spent helping people like Norman get to the hospital. The city was searched, then the river, then the bay. Fortunately, there weren't bodies floating around. There were very few deaths in Pascagoula.

Within days, the streets were cleared and building supplies began to arrive from other parts of the state. People, such as Paul, began the rebuilding process. Tina returned home, fully recovered, and reunited with Jamie. She and Hunter began spending time together.

Horn Island is an uninhabited island about twelve miles south of Pascagoula. Weeks later, when he felt as though it was safe to take a boat there, Hunter took Tina and Jamie there to spend a day enjoying the sugar-white sand and emerald surf. The water was still warm in September, but they had the island all to themselves. This was when Hunter proposed to Tina.

The wedding was the next spring. I will never forget the joy of hearing Hunter saying his vows to Tina, then on his knees pledging vows to Jamie to be a loving and faithful father as well as a husband to his mother.

Norman Ruble

Little Boy Surveys Home after Katrina

The Eye of Katrina before landfall

Chapter 11: Meant to Live

The helicopter was flying low, just above the trees as it approached a clearing where Viet Cong guerrillas were known to have set up camp. Dale was sitting on the platform inside the helicopter, but the rest of his body was more outside than inside. His legs dangled freely, and his head and torso leaned forward so he could get a good shot at the enemy. Another door gunner was doing the same on the other side of the Helicopter. There were three other American soldiers, including the pilot, who were fully inside the cockpit. Dale recalled the irony of enjoying the remarkable beauty of the lush green leaves scattering in the wind as the helicopter blades whirled by, combined with the sick feeling that he was about to kill other human beings or be killed.

Suddenly the forest opened to the clearing below. Dale looked through his scope to find his target. To his surprise, the Viet Cong was ready for them. This was expected to be a surprise attack. Before he could process what was occurring, a rocket-propelled grenade was launched into the air, aimed directly at the cockpit. Dale saw the plumb of smoke and heard the hissing of the rocket just before the missile penetrated the Helicopter's windshield. The loud explosion ruptured one of his eardrums, but other than in his ears, he felt no pain. The Helicopter began to spin out of control. Dale was trained for this situation to stay in the helicopter, all the way to the ground, but his instincts took control, and he unstrapped his seat belt and jumped.

He could feel tree leaves and limbs striking his face and body as he fell, each one slowing his descent. The last limb nearly stopped his fall entirely, allowing him to land safely on the ground. Instinctively, he rolled over onto his belly, lying flat so as not to be easily seen. Despite having an injured eardrum, he heard the explosion of the helicopter crashing to the ground. After the sound of the explosion faded, he could hear the yelps of the Viet Cong celebrating their victory. He thought for a moment what they might do to him if they found him, and that image was enough to stir him into action. If he could hear them, they could hear him, and if they could hear him, they could see him if he stood – he rationalized. He rolled toward the downward slope of the hill where he had landed. Once shielded from sight by the hill, he stood and ran as fast as he could. Shots were heard being fired behind him, but he was unsure if they were being fired at him or toward the sky in celebration. At one point, he had to climb a hill. Knowing this would make him visible for a great distance, he looked around for a better option. There was none. Once he finished his climb, he looked back and, in the distance, he could see the enemy was pursuing him. One pointed his way. They had seen him. His heart raced and he sprinted as fast as he could through the forest.

His heart pounded as he ran, not knowing where he was

going. He may have been running directly into more enemy forces for all he knew, for he hadn't the time or resources to ascertain his location. He fell more than once, but he had no time to think about whether he was hurt so he sprang to his feet each time and ran some more. Suddenly the forest opened to a flat grassy field. He could hear the Viet Cong pursuing him, causing him to realize that they would certainly reach this field before he made it to the forest on the other side. Realizing he had no better choice, he began sprinting across the field. The Viet Cong saw him and began firing when he was about three-quarters away from the tree line in front of him. The sound of bullets buzzing by may have been his imagination, but he heard them, nonetheless. Still running, he began to pray that if he were to get shot, for it to be a headshot so he would die quickly.

With each step, he got closer to the woods in front of him. Then suddenly, he noticed movement in front of him. Even with the sweat dripping in his eyes, and the shaking vision caused by his footsteps pounding the earth, he recognized human figures among the trees. His pace slowed slightly, for he feared he was running directly into the arms of the North Vietnamese army. The people in the woods in front of him began firing their rifles in his direction. Instinctively, he dropped to the ground. Soldiers appeared, continuously firing their rifles, but Dale could tell they weren't firing at him, they were firing past him. They were

American soldiers! He had been rescued!

While lying in a military hospital bed two days later, Dale learned later that everyone aboard the helicopter died in the fiery crash. He hadn't known those guys for long or very well but based on the little time he had with them, he considered them likable. He had trouble keeping the images of their faces from his mind. Inexplicably, to Dale, he felt guilty about being the sole survivor. He felt as if he had done something wrong by not perishing with them. Physically, he wasn't injured severely. He had a minor concussion, some cuts, and bruises, and was dehydrated when he was first admitted. Nevertheless, Dale expected to be released from the army when he recovered, which he considered some consolation for the trauma he was suffering. Each time he closed his eyes to sleep, he envisioned an image of his fallen mates. He tried to push them out of his mind with thoughts of his mother and father back on their farm in Nebraska.

Dale reported to his commanding officer upon being discharged from the hospital and learned he was not going home but was assigned to another team to serve as a door gunner again! He thought he might get sick and vomit on his CO upon hearing the news. He tried to convince his superiors that he wasn't ready to resume duties, but they weren't interested in his mental status.

When he met his new crewmates, Dale would not look them in the eyes and avoided looking at their faces. He thought he would know them by their voices exclusively, but he was wrong. Each time his helicopter lifted into the air, Dale couldn't restrain himself from looking at each one of them, thinking how this might be their last moments alive. Their missions were the most dangerous, for they weren't there to rescue anyone or deliver materials. They were there to provide air cover for ground troops, or to take out the enemy in remote areas. They were always shooting and getting shot at. The sound of bullets hitting the bottom of the helicopter was heard on most sorties. There were several times ground-to-air missiles were fired at their helicopter, the same type that brought down his previous crew, but the skilled pilot avoided them by making evasive maneuvers. But the memory of the deadly sortie which took the lives of his fellow crewmates returned with each plumb of smoke coming from the ground. Dale can't recall how much time passed or how many sorties he went on before his final journey with this crew.

The helicopter was flying fast at about a thousand feet in the air as they approached their target on the ground when Dale recognized the plumb of smoke and the hissing of the rocket as it moved rapidly toward their helicopter from the ground. The pilot maneuvered the helicopter to evade the missile as he had successfully done many times, but this time the rocket struck the helicopter's mast, detaching the rotor blades. The helicopter began to drop "like a rock" and Dale responded instinctively exactly as he had before. He jumped. The fall to the ground was much farther than his previous free fall. Dale guessed the helicopter was about seven or eight hundred feet in the air when he jumped. As before, he felt the tree limbs as he rocketed down toward Earth, but this time he didn't make it to the ground. He was stopped by a tree limb that impaled him. Facing the sky, he couldn't move. He was in terrible pain. The sharp limb which impaled him penetrated his body, puncturing a lung, and making breathing difficult. Passing in and out of consciousness, he lost track of time, but soon he heard voices in the jungle below him. They were the voices of the Vietnamese. He knew that they could see him if they looked up and would almost certainly shoot him. That is what he hoped for, a quick death by gunshots. There were horror stories about what happened to American soldiers who fell into enemy hands in Vietnam. Although his eyes were open to the bright blue sky above, he saw images of his family's farm in Nebraska as he prayed to God to end his suffering quickly and for him not to be taken alive by the Vietnamese. The voices below him faded away. They didn't look up and see him.

The sky above him grew darker as the sunset. The next time he woke the sky was filled with stars. Unsure of his injuries, he wondered how long he would continue to live. He couldn't tell how much blood he had lost or if he had internal bleeding. He couldn't move, so he slept most of the time. The following day he was awoken by rain falling on him. He opened his mouth and stuck out his tongue to capture as much of the water as he could. A day or two passed – Dale can't say for sure – when he heard voices below him once again. As the voices grew closer, he could recognize their language. They were Americans just below him. Knowing the only chance for his survival depended on them looking up and see him, he tried to call out to them, but his punctured lung wouldn't allow him enough air to yell, so tried to get their attention by moving his legs which dangled freely, but he could hardly feel them. Some of the soldiers' voices had moved on, but others were still nearby. They still had not looked up. Then he remembered the whistle in his pocket, issued by the military. He put it to his parched lips and tried to blow, but it hardly made a sound. After trying again and again, he could tell from their sound below the end of the line of soldiers was upon him. He had one last chance, so he inhaled the best he could with one lung and blew the whistle one last time. This time it made a squeaking sound just loud enough to gain the attention of one soldier who looked up and saw Dale dangling in the tree above.

Dale cannot recall how the soldiers got him down from the tree, but they did. Once again, he was transported to a military hospital, but this time the hospital was in Japan. His recovery took more than a month, for his injuries were more severe this time. Fortunately, none of his physical injuries were permanent, but when he learned that he was once again the sole survivor among his crew, he suffered mentally. Each time he was visited by a doctor or nurse, he told them, "I want to go home. Please tell them to send me home."

After being released from the hospital, he reported to his commanding officer. Dale asked if he could be sent home, but once again his CO denied his request. Dale attempted to plead but was cut short by his CO. Realizing he had no say in the matter, Dale told his CO that under no circumstances would he get on another helicopter. "You can court-martial me, or shoot me by firing squad, but I'm never getting on another helicopter."

Dale was assigned to infantry duty and never flew in a helicopter again. Months passed by without an incident, but one day while Dale was in a fox hole with another soldier, a messenger arrived and told Dale he was to report to his commanding officer for reasons unknown. The messenger replaced Dale in the fox hole. There had been no fighting that morning, but when Dale was only a few hundred yards away, he heard a loud explosion behind him. He turned around and saw the black cloud of smoke billowing from where the fox hole was — the one where he was just moments before. Had his replacement been just a few minutes later, Dale would have been killed by the blast.

Once again, he survived when others hadn't. Maybe his commanding officer took notice of Dale's history because he assigned Dale to non-combat duty this time. But his new job may have been worse than combat – to put dead soldiers into body bags and load them onto a plane to be flown back to the United States. Seeing one dead body after another, day after day, took a toll on Dale's mental condition. He finally had a nervous breakdown and was admitted to the military's psychiatric hospital. Eventually, he was discharged from the army and sent home to Nebraska.

The entire time he was in Vietnam, he imagined his return home would bring him peace and everything would return to normalcy, but Vietnam came home with him. Dale told me "It may have been my imagination, but I felt as if everyone treated me differently, looked at me differently as if I were a freak. I may have been acting strange, so maybe they were looking at me differently." He made one attempt to leave the farm and go into town, but he was so paranoid that he wouldn't leave the house again. He had difficulties having a normal conversation with anyone, not even his mother or father, so he retreated to his bedroom and hardly came out. At night, his sleep was filled with nightmares. Many years later Dale said, "I thought it was odd that I didn't have nightmares in Vietnam, but as soon as I got home,

I had them every night. You would think it would be the other way around."

Dale's mother pampered him at first, bringing his food to his bedroom, but his father refused to pamper him. One day his father had had enough of Dale "feeling sorry for himself" and ordered him out of his room. "Make yourself useful and go clean the barn!" His father yelled. Dale hadn't been outside for weeks and the sunshine felt good on his face. The wind was blowing, and the strong breeze was refreshing also. The barn was several hundred yards away from the house. It felt good to be outside. He enjoyed every step. After cleaning the barn, Dale began walking toward the house. The wind was blowing even more than before. Suddenly, off in the distance, behind the house, a huge funnel cloud formed, and it was moving directly toward the house where his parents were, and toward him! The tornado was moving quickly throwing dust and debris into the air. Dale watched with horror as the tornado leveled his parents' home. Having only seconds to react, he looked around for the lowest place to lie down. Nebraska is flat, and there wasn't a ditch near him, so fell flat, face down on the ground, and covered his head with his hands. The sound of the tornado passing over him was deafening, but he was unharmed when it passed. The barn behind him was leveled, but more frightening was the sight of his family's house having been removed to the slab. He said out loud, "not again" and began running toward the house with tear-filled eyes. With each step, he thought that once again he was going to be the sole survivor of a tragedy, but this time was even worse than any time before – his parents were involved. He wondered if he was cursed. The house was destroyed down to its foundation. There was no sign of his parents, not even a body. But suddenly he heard a banging noise. He went to where the source of the banging and began moving framing studs and debris, uncovering the storm shelter's door. The door swung open, and his father appeared, then his mother. They had survived too!

Dale hugged his parents tightly and they hugged back, but then for the first time since he was deployed to Vietnam, he broke down and cried for what seemed to him like a long time. He sobbed loudly too, and his mother said, "go ahead, cry it out of you." Dale said he "cried and cried and cried." When he finished crying his mother said, "It's all right Dale. The house can be rebuilt, and things can be replaced, but we are still here. God wasn't ready for us yet. He still has a plan for us."

About forty years later, Dale told me this story. He was hosting a barbeque for his son's baseball teammates and coaches and parents, of which I was one. Dale said, "That's when I realized that I was meant to live. I didn't know what God had planned for me, but I knew that I was meant to live to serve a purpose." He pointed at his son, Jay, and said, "Now I know. He is my purpose."

After hearing his story, I asked "has anything like that happened to you since?"

"No, not a single thing."

"In that case, I'm getting the hell away from you!" I joked and we laughed.

He continued, "In fact, after that day, I was able to live life again. I stopped having nightmares and was able to get a job and carry on conversations as a normal person. Once I realized the reason I survived all those events is that God had a purpose for me, I no longer felt guilt or shame."

Dale hadn't told many people his story and doesn't like to talk about it, and for that reason, his name has been changed. I was honored he felt close enough to me to share his story with me, and I believe his story is worth preserving.

Chapter 12: Impressing Children

Guilty. That is what I am. Guilty of trying to spoil my children. Unless you skipped the proceeding chapters, you probably figured out that I had a modest childhood and times were lean. Like most people of my time and circumstances, I wanted my children to have the things and experiences that I wanted but did not have as a child. This is likely the root cause of the entitlement attitude of the so-called Millennial generation, but more on that later.

Bailey loved trains. He loved trains before he could speak. He loved Thomas the Choo Choo the most. He would wake from a deep sleep whenever the car passed over train tracks and he would say in a sweet voice, "too too tane tacks?"

For his third or fourth birthday, I took him on a short, forty-five-minute trip aboard the local Amtrak train. The trip almost lasted much longer because when it came time to get off the train, Bailey took off running, darting between people and even under one person's legs – places that I couldn't go – determined to see where the train engineer shoveled coal into the fire. By the time that I caught up with him, the train had already begun moving as we stepped off just in time to keep from traveling all the way to Memphis.

A few years went by, and I decided that it was time for

another train ride, but this time the whole family would travel to a real destination; New Orleans. Bailey was about five or six and Anna was and still is twenty months younger. The Amtrak from Jackson to New Orleans is a lot of fun. It is long enough to feel as though you are really going somewhere, but not so long as to become tiresome. After checking into our room in New Orleans, we walked to Jackson Square, where street performers entertained us all. There are horse-drawn carriages that will take you on a site-seeing tour through the historic French Quarter. Despite the many times that I've been to New Orleans, I had never had that experience. This seemed like the perfect time. Surely the children will be impressed by riding in a horse-drawn carriage. They seemed to enjoy the ride. I did.

Next, we visited the IMAX theatre and the aquarium. From there, we boarded a historic river steamboat that took us down the Mississippi River to the Audubon Zoo, where they all axed for you. Anna sat in my lap and Bailey stood by my side looking at the sites as the steamboat's huge paddle wheel churned up the river water. "What do you think about this? Isn't this cool?" I asked them both. They both nodded.

The Audubon Zoo is an attraction that every child seems to enjoy, but a day at the zoo can drain a lot of energy from most people. Leaving the zoo, we climbed aboard one of the famous streetcars of New Orleans. The children had to have been impressed by the streetcar. They had never seen anything like this before – and the beautiful trees and huge homes, well it still impresses me, and I've seen St. Charles Street a million times.

We got off the streetcar at the closest point to our hotel, the Hilton Riverwalk. Anna was so exhausted that she could not walk, and I was too tired to carry her the two or three long blocks to the hotel, so I hailed a taxi. We climbed into the taxi which wreaked with stale cigarette smoke, alcohol, and who knows what else. The seats were nasty, it was hot, and the windows could not be lowered all the way. It was better than carrying Anna the distance, but I was glad to get out of that cab.

The following morning, we enjoyed watching balloon artists as we ate beignets at Cafe du Monde. As I sat there, reflecting on our fun-filled weekend, I wondered what impressed my children the most – the train ride, the horse-drawn carriage, the aquarium, the IMAX theater, the steamboat, the zoo, or the streetcar, so I asked them. "Of all of the things that you did while we have been in New Orleans, what has been the most fun thing that you've done?"

Without hesitation, they both answered at once, "the taxi ride!"

ST. CHARLES
971

Chapter 13:

Lil' Wayne and the Princess

Anna has always been, and still is, my sweet little pretty precious, baby-darling-angel princess; she was aka the Princess of Breland. Birthdays have always been special to me. As humble as we were, my mother and father always tried to make a big deal about our birthdays. As I got older, I made my birthday my own special holiday. As a young man, I began celebrating my birthday days ahead and eventually for days after. In fact, since Independence Day is just three days later, I made a point to celebrate my birthday and Independence Day without a pause. I don't do that anymore, but I have tried to make birthdays special for my family.

On her sixth birthday, she went to school like any other day, but we surprised her by checking her out of class by mid-morning. She was even more surprised to see that Bailey was in the car. He had been checked out of school also. She had no idea what we were up to, and we wouldn't tell her. "Where are we going?" she would ask. "You will see when we get there," came our answer. We drove to the airport, checked in, and waited to board our flight. She never noticed the "to Orlando" posted just above her head while we waited. It wasn't until we got off the plane in Orlando that she realized that we were going to Disney World.

There was the Libby Lu makeup party when she was nine and others, but a sweet-sixteenth birthday is special. She deserved something to remember. The thing that she wanted to do the most was to go to a Lil' Wayne concert.

"Little Wayne? Who is Little Wayne?" I asked.

"Not Little Wayne, Lil' Wayne! He is like the biggest star ever," she explained.

I had never heard of Lil' Wayne, and I try to stay tuned-in to the hip-music scene. I am what one might call a groovy guy, but this one had slipped by me.

"What does he sing? Maybe I've heard his songs and didn't pay attention to the singer's name."

Anna hesitated to answer. She knew, and knows, that there is only one type of music that I truly do not like and that is rap music. There are some rap songs that I think are ok, but the ones that have vulgar words and hateful messages are disgusting to me. She beat around the bush and tried to camouflage her answer until there was no way around it, Lil' Wayne is a rapper!

"What! Rap music? Do you want to go to a rap concert? When did you start liking rap music? I thought you liked Stevie Nicks."

"I do like Stevie Nicks, Dad. I like all sorts of music, but I really like Lil' Wayne, and if you listened to him with an open mind, you would like him too."

"Well, isn't there something else that you would like to do for your birthday; like go to the beach or something?"

"No Dad, I really want to go to see Lil' Wayne. I've been wanting to for a long time, but I understand if you don't want to take me," she said.

The way she said that gave me the idea that she might go with or without me, so I asked, "Where is the concert?"

"It's in New Orleans." The most dangerous city in America.

Instantly images of the Crips and Bloods shooting at one another with my sweet princess caught in the crossfire flooded my brain. Right or wrong, I associate rap music with gun-toting, knife-wielding, gangstas high on something that makes them want to use guns and knives, and New Orleans is the most dangerous city this side of Syria. Don't get me wrong, I love New Orleans, especially the Saints, but it has always been known as a very dangerous city.

"New Orleans! Oh my God! Do you want to go to a rap concert in New Orleans for your birthday? Are you tired of having birthdays or something?"

"Yes, Dad. Where else would he play? He is too big to play around here, and where else would he play for his farewell tour? He *is* from New Orleans."

"Farewell tour? Where is he going?"

"To prison… but he was framed… for having a marijuana cigarette."

Was she testing me? How did she morph into a person who likes rap music without my having noticed? It had to be her mother's fault. "Well, play some of his music so that I can see if I can tolerate it for a few hours."

"You don't have to go with me, Dad. I am sixteen years old. I can go with one of my friends. I just need you to take us down there."

"There is no possibility that my sixteen-year-old daughter is going to a rap concert, or any concert in New Orleans, without me being there to protect you."

She connected her cell phone to my car's speakers and played a Lil' Wayne song. It wasn't too bad, but I am sure that she picked the tamest song of all for my first exposure.

She wanted for her birthday more than anything else to see Lil Wayne, so I agreed that she could go with a friend, so long as I went with them as well. She agreed and thanked me profusely.

The idea worried me. I could see a thousand scenarios that could evolve into something bad. Not knowing anything at all about Lil' Wayne or his followers, I perceived that I would be the only old white guy there for sure, so I had to come up with a plan to look less conspicuous. We had to blend in so that the Crypts and the Bloods wouldn't notice us.

As it turned out, Anna's friend couldn't make it, so just the two of us went. When arrived at the concert hall, I was wearing old blue jeans with holes, a hoody, a baseball cap turned sideways, and even sported some bling bling; but Anna was dressed like a normal, middle-class suburbanite – she was sure to stand out like a sore thumb!

"I will be all right, Dad, I promise," she assured me.

There was a huge crowd of people – thousands – even with tickets costing $100 a pop. We made our way to the seats. Anna wanted a soft drink, but I was concerned about leaving her alone among the gangstas.

"I will be all right, Dad. Do you see any gangstas?"

I looked around and for the first time noticed that everyone around looked like middle-class suburbanites, so I left her there while I made my way to the concession stand. Standing in line ahead of me was this young, attractive black couple. Both were well dressed and well groomed. She wore tasteful jewelry and had stylish hair. He wore cardigan sweater and dress slacks; was clean-shaven and had a conservative haircut.

Not intending to eavesdrop, I hear the young man ask in the most articulate manner, "So, how do you think you did on your trigonometry test?"

His friend replied in equally proficient articulation, "I think that I made an A, but that professor is really hard, so we shall see."

This surprised me because, I can't even spell trigonometry without a spell check, and that was the last thing that I expected to be discussed at a gangsta concert.

I looked around at the crowd and realized that I was the only gangsta in the house!

Lesson learned. Don't stereotype.

Chapter 14: The Help

You may have read the book or more likely seen the movie, *The Help*. The author grew up in a home across the street from my children's grandparents' home, which looks suspiciously like the home in the movie in which the antagonist Hilly lived and may have served as inspiration for the book. The grandparents' home has his and her water closets in the garage, but not at all like those in the movie. The water closets in the movie were unairconditioned, unpainted, and undecorated. The real-life bathrooms are not only air-conditioned but decorated with granite countertops, ceramic tiled floors, showers, expensive fixtures, and hardware – all fitting for an upscale home. I recall once when one person was at the grandparents' home, inquiring about the outdoor water closets.

"Do you allow your help to use the bathrooms in the house?" she asked.

"Of course, we do, why do you ask?" was the owner's response.

"Why do you have bathrooms in the garage, if not for the help?"

She explained that the water closets were for anyone who did not want to go through the house to use the bathrooms, which might include those enjoying the swimming pool or the yard man.

"Oh, so it's for the yard man? Is he not allowed to use the bathroom in the house?"

"Yes, he can, but why would he want to if he has one much more convenient to him in the garage?"

That is a brief summary of the conversation that took place in the 1990s, and to my knowledge, the subject never came up again until years later when the book was written.

Pascagoula, MS 1975

I had just hopped into Starlie's car for my ride home from the football game. The effects of adrenaline from the excitement of great performance and victory fueled my emotions. I began to ask her if she saw me make that one fantastic play, probably a quarterback sack. She replied, "Of course I did. My eyes never left you during the entire game. Even when you were on the sideline."

For a moment, I felt sad for her. She had never and will never experience the thrill and excitement of playing football. She recognized my momentary sadness and asked me to explain what I was thinking, so I did.

"Would you believe that I enjoy watching you play football, as much as you enjoy playing, maybe even more?"

"Impossible! I love playing football more than anything. You just think that because you don't understand, since you never played."

"Maybe you don't understand how I can enjoy watching your love life because you've never had a son. If you are lucky, you will have a son one day, and then you will understand."

Madison, MS 2010

Standing in the cold, wind-driven rain, in the football stands, somewhere around the forty-yard line, I remembered that conversation from 35 years prior, as clear as if it had been the day before. Mama was right!

I could see my son's face after he removed his helmet, jogging toward the sideline with the rest of the defense, with a huge smile on his face. He had just made a spectacular play, a quarterback sack! Despite the rain, there were stars that could be seen in the sky. I looked up, hoping that my mother was looking down and could read my mind. Yes, Mama, you were right. I couldn't believe it until I experienced it for myself, but I actually got more joy out of watching my son play than I had playing for all those years, including three undefeated teams and two state championships. Madison Central High School was a new school but has quickly become one of the biggest in Mississippi. Their football program has also quickly become one of the elite programs in the state. There had only been one school in Mississippi that kept the Madison Central Jaguars from going to the state championship all four of my son's high school years – South Panola, which was literally the No. 1 ranked team in the nation, having a ten-year winning streak with no losses, was the obstacle his freshman, sophomore, and junior seasons.

Bailey's senior year was special. His final game of the season was the state semi-final championship game against Olive Branch High School. Yep, Madison Central finally beat South Panola his senior season. Now, once again, there was only one game more to win to make it to the state championship.

The game was at least a three-hour drive away, so the school chartered a bus for anyone who needed transportation to the game, but I had my own transportation. I got there early so that I could get the best seat available. This would be the last time that I enjoyed this ritual and the last time that I might see many of the people who were there week after week to watch our boys play. Like so many proud fathers of football stars, I wore a replica of my son's jersey. His number was 78, and our name was stitched on the back above the numbers. There was another man there wearing the same jersey. His name is James.

He is the yardman for my son's grandparents.

The same grandparents who own the home and likely inspired *The Help*.

James never missed any of my son's home football games. He even made it to most of the away games that didn't require a long drive. Sitting beside James was his wife. They paid $50 to ride the chartered bus to the game. That is no small amount for a person of modest means. I sat next to James and told him that I was glad to see him.

"I wouldn't have missed this one for anything. No sir: I wasn't going to miss my boy playing a game this important," he said with enthusiasm.

"If I had known that you were coming, you could have ridden with me."

"That's no problem. We wanted to ride the bus," he said.

James has been the yardman for the same family for many years. Linda has worked for the same family as their housekeeper for about thirty years. People don't work for the same employer for twenty and thirty years if they are unhappy. They are more than just help; they have become part of the family.

You wouldn't think that possible if you saw the movie,

which was based on a book, possibly inspired by these very people.

Many people who have never lived in the South, think that modern-day Mississippi is no different than the depictions in the movies. This seems like an opportunity for me to clear up some misconceptions and defend my state's honor.

I may not know much about much, but I know m u c h a b o u t Mississippi. I've lived and worked in the state my entire life. My father, grandfather, great-grandfather, and great-great-grandfather were all born and lived in Mississippi. My great-great-grandfather fought for the Confederacy, but he didn't own slaves and didn't fight to preserve slavery. He fought because he was conscripted on his 18th birthday when the war was half over, and fighting was better than getting hanged for not fighting.

If the KKK was actively recruiting new members, I probably would have heard from them by now. I haven't. I've never met anyone who knows anyone in the KKK. I've met all sorts of people, from all walks of life, but I've never met a single person who claimed to be a member of a white supremacist group or spoke favorably of them.

Gossip is the number one source of entertainment in Mississippi, since we don't have professional sports teams, and you know what they say about scorned women. There are few men who haven't scorned at least one woman over the years. If a scorned woman knew her ex was in the KKK, she would have told everyone who would listen and then some. If the KKK existed in Mississippi beyond a lonely sociopath living on an isolated dirt road somewhere, I think that I would have crossed paths with someone who knows someone in the KKK by now. Yet, my life experiences have me convinced that Americans have become less racist with each generation.

Like I said before, Morgan Freeman said, "If you want to end racism, stop talking about it." He is right. I believe if politicians, the media, and especially the movie and television industry, stopped perpetuating the narrative that all southern white folks are hateful racists and all blacks should not trust their fellow citizens, racism would likely stop being a major political issue, and Americans would be far more united, and there would be less violence.

Mama (Starlie) and Me in 1975

Chapter 15: Ghost of Mississippi

I once owned a home backing up to an old cemetery, with dates on headstones going back to the early 1800s. People would ask if I were nervous about living so close to a graveyard. It didn't bother me at all. In fact, my family went all out for Halloween each year by creating a spooky trail that started by leading the trick-or-treaters through the side courtyard. As kids entered the New Orleans-styled courtyard the strobe lights reflected through the fog machine's artificial mist. The faux rocks in the flower beds were speakers which played scary soundtracks from movies such as *Psycho* and *Friday the 13th*.

After ducking under cobwebs adorning plastic spiders and fully inside the courtyard, children could see the two (fake) headstones strategically placed so well that many children asked if we really had buried bodies there. There were fake bones and other Halloween decorations such as a full-sized witch made of stuffing which sat in the rocking chair underneath the porch.

Through the next gate at the other end of the courtyard was a black slag trail that led through the backyard to the other side of the house. Trick-or-treaters' eyes were focused on the left because the cemetery could be seen through the rails of the wrought iron fence. If that weren't bad enough, there would be two full-sized skeletons holding onto the fence, as if attempting to climb over into my yard. Since their eyes were always focused on the rear fence, they never noticed my son, dressed as a zombie or some other scary costume, who would hide behind the bushes which lined the back of the house. He would jump out at the last second and scare the snickers bars right out of those kiddos. Other than Halloween, our house was pretty much absent the paranormal events, except for that one time:

Around 8 a.m. one weekday in mid-April 2004, I was alone in the house for about fifteen minutes or so when I opened the house door leading into the enclosed garage. I noticed that the dome light was on in my car. My first thought was that I had left the light on all night long and now my car might not start making me late for the scheduled appointment with my construction supervisor and building supply representative. Before I could reach my car to investigate, the light went off. As I processed that information, I realized fifteen minutes or so had passed since my family had departed. All three garage doors were closed, so I considered the possibility that someone had just opened my car door. I looked around cautiously, but no one was around. I opened the car door and set the timer clock on my phone to learn how long the light stayed on after the car door was opened and closed...seven seconds.

Seven seconds? It takes nearly that long for the garage doors to close, which I concluded meant that whoever opened my car door was still in the garage! The hair stood up on the back of my neck. I'm not a violent person, wouldn't hurt a flea, or even kill a deer, but if someone poses a threat to me or my family, I will do what I must do, so I instinctively picked up a nearby baseball bat that hung out with the rest of my son's baseball gear, and lifted it in the head-bashing position. I walked slowly to the storage doors and flung them open, fully prepared to do the Al Capone thing, but no one was there. I quickly swiveled my body thinking that I was being approached from behind, but no one was there either. I looked under the car, in the trunk, and all around, but no one was there. Then I realized that this was a mystery that I had no time for; I had a business to run, so I put down the baseball bat, re-entered the house, leaving the door to the garage open for some reason, and walked through the kitchen to an office nook where a desktop computer and chair awaited. I sat down and opened up my emails and began to compose one to myself – I have an excellent long term memory, but I have difficulty with short term memory because I try to stuff too much info into a small space. Knowing that about myself, I felt inclined to email myself a reminder about some important things to discuss with my construction team, because the distraction in the garage increased the chances of my forgetting before I could get to the office.

I was engrossed in the drafting of the email when I heard

a woman's laugh. My family knows that when I am focused on something, like typing on the computer, I can't hear anything but my thoughts, not even when someone speaks directly to me; but maybe because I was already a little unnerved by the thought that I was prepared to crush a bad guys skull open only moments before, it occurred to me that the laughter sounded as if it came from inside the house!

I sprang up from my chair and rushed to the open door and looked in the garage, but no one was there. I looked up the staircase but didn't go up because the laughter was too clear to have come from upstairs; no one was seen standing on the stairs. I walked around the corner to the hallway leading toward my home-office; no one there. I checked my bedroom next and once again, no one was there.

I stood perplexed in the doorway of my bedroom and hallway, wondering if I had imagined hearing the laugh. I was focused on the email and maybe, I was hearing things. Hmmm. But suddenly, just as I was about to convince myself that I was hearing things...there it was again – clear as a bell – a woman's laughter! I darted down the hall and spun around the corner to the foot of the stairs where I could see the entire kitchen, keeping room and up the stairs. No one was there, but I know that I heard her loud and clear, so I called out with a chuckle in my voice, "Ok, ok, you've had your fun, I know you are there, come on down."

But no one answered. I couldn't hear a sound. I walked up the stairs, because from where I had been standing, it sounded as if it came from just around the corner, where the stairs were located. Once upstairs, I checked every room, but no one was anywhere to be found. There were no televisions or radios playing, or any other electronics. I walked back downstairs, and then I heard it again. This time it sounded like it came from upstairs where I had just looked. It was as if she was laughing because I couldn't find her. Without going into an entirely different story, there had been an event that caused me to wonder if a real-life psycho killer might be in my house, so I decided it was time to call for backup.

My brother and his wife lived down the street, so I called him and asked, "Please come to my house for a minute. I need you to check something out."

"I don't mind, but can't you tell me what it is first?"

"No, I would rather tell you when you get here."

"Now you have to tell me or I'm not coming."

"Ok, don't tell anyone, but I think there might be someone in my house."

"What makes you think that?"

"Can't you just come here?"

"No, not until you tell me why. I need to know whether to bring my gun."

"Ok, ok, you might think that I'm crazy, but I keep hearing a woman's laughter, and I can't find her, so I think she is hiding in the house."

"A woman is laughing at you?"

"Yes," I said, knowing one of his famous one-liners was coming.

"Are you naked?" he said with a laugh.

"Would you please just come here? And don't say anything to anyone"

He showed up with his wife, who couldn't keep a secret if she were alone on a deserted island. I told them the story, but the entire time they were there, we heard no laughter, except for my brother and his wife as they cracked one joke after another at my expense.

Embarrassed, I thanked them for coming, and began to question my own sanity. I called my supervisor and sales rep and asked them to come to my house instead of my office for the meeting due to the delay.

When they arrived, they could tell that I was not my usual self, so I told them an abbreviated version of the story. They looked at each other simultaneously then back at me as if I were insane. If I hadn't been the boss and customer, they probably would have said so.

We began to study house plans when I heard the woman's laugh once again. "Did y'all hear that?" I asked.

They both confirmed that they heard it and agreed that it came from inside of the house. The three of us spread out quickly into different rooms, but like before, we found no one. Then the questions came: "Do your children have a toy that makes a laughing sound? Is there an electronic game in the house? Did the laughter sound the same each time? How often have you heard the sound?"

"No, no, no, and no set pattern that I could ascertain."

I called my brother again because I wanted him to hear from these other two men to prove my sanity. He returned by himself, and the other two men confirmed that they had heard it too, but my brother was still skeptical. Then we all heard it again, and again, and again.

We are all home builders, so we know a thing or two about a thing or two when it comes to homes. We turned off all the power to the house to rule out electronic devices. We used walkie talkies to communicate with one another as we covered every inch of the house, literally top to bottom in search of the source of laugher. We went into the attic, on top of the roof, inspected the fireplace chimney and even inside the dishwasher and oven. We wrote down the times that we heard the laughter to see if there was a pattern.

The laugh sounded differently each time. Sometimes it was more of a chuckle or a weak laugh, and at other times, it was a roaring laugh. We could not tell where it was coming from. We all agreed that at times it seemed to come from upstairs, and at other times it seemed to come from around the corner in the hallway, and at other times it sounded as if she were standing right next to us as she laughed. It truly sounded as if someone was laughing at us because we couldn't find her.

About two and a half hours later, it stopped, and I never heard the laugh again. I confirmed with my children that they did not have a game that produced laughter, but I didn't tell them this story until we no longer lived there. I shouldn't admit this, but although I never heard her laugh again, there were a few times when I was home alone, and I called out, "Hello? Is anyone there?"

Chapter 16: The Cruise from Hell

Mama said, "Don't make the mistake that I did. Don't wait to do the things that you want to do. If you want to travel, for example, travel. Don't wait until you retire, or until you think you can afford it. Do it." So, I did.

When Bailey and Anna were about five and six years old, we took a trip to New York City. We went to the top of the World Trade Center, and the Empire State Building and did lots of other things. By the time we boarded the plane for the return trip, we were exhausted and ready to get home.

We heard the flight attendant announce "Attention everyone, we have a slight problem. This plane is overbooked, and we cannot depart until four passengers get off the plane. Do we have any volunteers?"

She waited for a response, but there was none, so she continued. "Let me repeat, we must have four passengers get off this plane or we cannot depart. The airlines will reimburse you for your tickets and put you on the next flight home if you will volunteer to remove yourself from this flight."

I looked over at my wife, who sat next to Bailey in the seats across the aisle that separated us. She signaled with her eyes that she was not in the mood to volunteer. Neither was I, besides, I had to get back to work the next day. So, we just sat there, unresponsive to the flight attendant's plea for volunteers.

Her offer became more generous. "We will *not only* reimburse you for your tickets, but we will put you up in a hotel at our expense and buy your dinner tonight if you volunteer to get off this plane. I repeat we need four people to volunteer!"

When we ignored that plea, she said, "Ok, I just got word from the airlines that we will not only give you everything that I've mentioned before, but we will provide you with a free round-trip ticket to anywhere in North America."

My wife could tell that my interest had piqued so she began shaking her head "no."

With a more desperate tone, the flight attendant said, "We really must have four people depart this plane or we cannot go anywhere, so we are willing to reimburse you for your tickets, provide you with a free trip home on the next flight, plus pay for your dinner and hotel room if that next flight is tomorrow, and give you two free round trip tickets for each of you, which you have up to a full year to use. To be clear, that is eight, round trip tickets, which can be used anywhere in North America for a whole year!"

Now I was so curious that I could not keep quiet. I had to

ask, "are these transferable?"

"What do you mean, sir?" she asked.

My wife was squirming in her seat to get my attention and I could hear her whispering, but not so quietly, "no, no! We've got to get home!"

But I had gone too far with my question. "I mean, do each of us have to use the tickets or could we use some of them to take friends or other family members on trips?"

While holding the microphone to her mouth so that everyone could hear her response, she said, "Sir, let me put it this way. Almost everyone on this plane is on a school field trip. They are either minors or their chaperones, so they cannot be separated. For that reason, this airline is so desperate to get four people off this plane, they will agree to almost anything. By the way, how many are in your party?"

Then she pointed the microphone to my lips so that everyone could hear my reply, which was, sheepishly, "Four."

The rest of the passengers, who had been amazingly patient up until now began yelling, "Get off of this plane!"

Even though my wife gave me the I-am-going-to- strangle-you-later look, I realized that we had to get off this plane. I decided to make the most of the opportunity, hoping that if I negotiated a fabulous deal, she might not actually strangle me. "Would the airline be willing to give us twelve round trip tickets to anywhere in North America that are transferable, and not have a one-year expiration, but say, five-year expiration?"

Over the crowd's chanting, "Get off, get off," I heard the flight attendant say, "Probably so, but let me confirm." While she was in the cockpit, apparently confirming acceptance of my offer, my wife let me know that she did not approve of my decision. I tried to explain to her that we had no choice but to get off the plane, so we may have at least made it worth our while.

"Yes. The airline agreed to your terms," she said.

"Twelve, transferable, round-trip tickets to anywhere in North America, with five-year expiration, plus dinner and a hotel tonight?"

"Yes, that's right sir."

"Can I have that in writing?"

"Yes, I will put that in writing for you if you tell me right now that you agree to these terms. Otherwise, we are going to cancel this flight!"

"I agree!"

My wife's body began to spasm and the flight attendant began writing out the agreement.

"Just for the record," I asked, "are we the only four people on this plane who are not with the school field trip?"

"Yes, sir, that is correct. You are the only ones who are not on the field trip," she said as holding the microphone to her lips.

Now I felt vindicated and had a good defense for not being strangled by the wife.

Maybe I am a conspiracy theorist, but I suspect the airline tried to get a little revenge on us that night. They gave us free transportation from the Newark airport to the hotel – make that motel. The entry door was made of such thin plywood, I could have put my fist through, and it did not have so much as a deadbolt lock. The only way to lock the door was by pushing and turning the doorknob. Knowing how easy that these locks can be opened with a credit card, or so I've been told, I used one of the beds to block the door when we went to sleep that night. The dinner that night was at a Captain D's.

The free flight home the next day was unusual as well. A typical journey home would be New York to Atlanta, then on to Jackson, but this trip took us to Minneapolis, then Memphis, then Jackson. We were home eighteen hours later. Anna fell asleep on the plane to Minneapolis and did not wake until she got home. That means that I carried her off and on planes and through three airports, along with handling luggage. My back is still out of whack.

The good news is, that we got to go on some fun trips thanks to Delta Airlines. We made a deal with few of our friends in which we provided the airfare, and they provided the accommodations to Key West and Cozumel. It became an annual tradition among us to go on an all-adult vacation in February. We kept up this tradition even was time to experience a cruise.

A cold, wintery day in February 2001, my wife and I met up with two other couples in New Orleans to take a cruise ship to Cozumel. The designated preboarding meeting place was TGI Fridays. This is where we solidified our plans for the evening. It was sleeting outside, so we agreed that we would all do our own thing until eight o'clock that evening, at which time we would meet for dinner.

While having dinner, I felt a slight bump like the bump you feel or hear when an air-conditioning system starts up at times. It was hardly noticeable, and I would never have thought about it again had it not been for what happened next. The lights went dark a few seconds later. It was so dark that I couldn't see my hand in front of my eyes. I tried. This was before smartphones, so people still used lighters and matches instead of cell phone flashlights in such situations. A few lighters began illuminating the room, but as suddenly as the lights went dark, they were back on again, followed by the most pleasant Englishman's voice coming from the ship's intercom speakers: "Hello passengers. I am certain that you noticed that we had a momentary power outage. Not to worry. The power has been totally restored and the cause of the event has been corrected, and we are sure to have no such reoccurrence. Enjoy the rest of your cruise."

We were satisfied with the explanation, so we continued our meal. The incident left our mines and would never have been thought of again had it not been for what happened next.

Since the ship was still in the Mississippi River, and the weather was cold and sleeting, we all retired to our cabins immediately after dinner. That suited me just fine because I was anxious to wake up early and enjoy the sunrise. If you have never seen a sunrise over the open water, especially a sunrise over waters of the Gulf of Mexico or the Caribbean, then you need to take my mother's advice and do it. Don't wait. Do it.

When I began to stir, early the next morning, my wife said to me, "We aren't moving."

"What do you mean, not moving?" I asked, still half asleep.

"This ship is not moving."

"Oh. No, you are mistaken. This is such a big ship; you just don't feel the waves."

"No. I am certain that this ship has not moved for hours."

"Well then, I will just have to investigate. I will return with coffee and a report."

With that I sprang out of bed, slipped on some clothes, and made my way to the boat's nearest side rail, expecting to see the beautiful expanse of the Gulf of Mexico, but instead, I saw...a trailer park. I looked straight down, and I saw, sitting on a pier with a cane pole in his hand, a man with a straw hat, starring back up at me. We had run aground on the bank of the Mississippi River.

After giving the report to my wife, we met our friends for breakfast. The television was tuned to CNN, which was reporting on us. The view of our ship was being broadcast from a news camera about a helicopter flying above us. It was then that we heard the voice once again, "Hello passengers. By now you've likely noticed that we have slightly run aground. Not to worry, the Coast Guard is currently inspecting the ship as they are required, and early reports are that there is no damage, and we will be on our way shortly. In the meantime, please enjoy the all-you-can-eat breakfast buffet."

We were on our way shortly thereafter – eight hours later! The voice spoke to us once again.

"Hello passengers. Due to the slight delay that we had earlier, the captain has decided to make a slight variation in our itinerary. Instead of traveling to Cozumel, we will be traveling to Key West instead. Not to worry. Key West is lovely this time of year and has as much or more to offer you than Cozumel. This decision was made so that you will have more time to enjoy yourself than if we had continued onward to Cozumel. Remember passengers, it's more about the journey than the destination anyway, so enjoy your travels. By the way. Don't forget to visit the casino where we have double slots and half-priced drinks during happy hour."

We finally made it out of the Mississippi River and into the open waters of the Gulf of Mexico. No more watching. The sky was filled with the thick wintery cumulous clouds, so it was unpleasant to be outdoors. That left only two things to do – drink or gamble. I chose to do both. That became boring after a couple of hours, so I decided to meet up with the others in our group to see what they were doing for entertainment. A couple of them had returned to their cabins, hoping for a nap, but the ship's rocking motion made them seasick.

We were about an hour from Key West when the sun came out and the temperature rose to the mid-seventies. Finally, we were in the tropics. Like a kid who just got out of school for the summer vacation, we hurriedly put on our bathing suits and were poolside with rum daiquiris and such in record time. Then, we heard the voice again.

"Hello passengers. As you surely know, we shall be docking shortly in beautiful Key West, Florida. Due to the previous interruption, we must have an abbreviated visit, so you have one hour to enjoy the sights and sounds before boarding for the return trip home. Please be advised that we must depart with or without you if you have not returned in one hour. Not to worry though, there are many things to see and do, right there in the harbor next to where we shall be docking."

Unsure that I heard the voice correctly, we all asked the same question – "Did he say that we had only one hour in Key West?"

Once I got over the surprise of that announcement, I began to suspect that something was not quite right. Accounting for the time lost while being stuck in the Mississippi, we should still have more time than just an hour to explore Key West.

Our group had been to Key West the previous year, by plane, so we knew where we wanted to spend our one hour – Sloppy Joes. Once there, we had two or three drinks and called our children and instructed them how to see us on Sloppy Joe's web cam. That was a big deal back then. With modern technology, there is no longer such a novelty as seeing someone live via camera from remote places.

We returned to the ship within the allotted time. An hour later, we had traveled out of the sunny tropics back to the cloudy, dreary wintery north. In total, we had three whole hours of sunshine the entire trip. Instead of spending more money on booze or gambling, I decided to go to my cabin and take a nap. As I lay there, I could feel the gentle rocking of the boat and could see how so many of the others had gotten seasick. The good Lord blessed me such, that I have never been seasick. I enjoy the rocking motion of the sea. Suddenly I thought, "that must have been a big wave" because the back-and-forth rhythm was interrupted with a longer and deeper tilting of the ship to one side – in the direction away from the wall and towards the door. Then the ship rocked back in the other direction, toward the wall, then back again, but this time, the depth and duration were such that my bed moved across the floor toward the door, slowly and slightly, but significant enough to notice. The ship rocked back in the other direction. The ship began to rock again. This time the bed started sliding slowly away from the wall for two or three seconds – I expected it to stop and reversed directions at any moment – but then suddenly, the entire bed flipped over dumping me onto the floor. The room's floor was tilted at about a forty-five-degree angle. I heard glass breaking outside of my cabin and could hear people screaming in terror.

I made my way over and opened the door, which was not easy considering that I had to pull it uphill against gravity while trying not to fall forward. Peering into the hall, I saw a crewman walking, using one hand against the wall to brace himself. Before I could speak, more doors began to open with peering heads.

Someone asked, "What is going on?"

The crewman answered, "Stay in your rooms until you hear instructions otherwise."

I did as he instructed, but then began thinking of my wife and friends, wondering what their circumstances were. I had to investigate, but first I had to go to the bathroom. When you gotta go, you gotta go. For you to understand the magnitude of how much the ship was listing, I had to aim at the sink to hit the correct target. While that was taking place – I heard the voice again.

"Hello passengers. By now I am certain that you've noticed the ship is listing slightly a bit. Not to worry, the captain is aware of the cause and is taking corrective measures. The situation should return to normal shortly. In the meantime, I want to remind those of you who are using the stairs to hold on tightly to the handrails."

The vision of my wife and friends holding onto the handrails with a thirty-foot drop below them, as you might have seen in the movie *The Poseidon Adventure*, appeared vividly to me. I had to find them. Making my way down the slanted hall was an eerie experience. I'm not one to panic, but I must say that the next crewman that I encountered certainly didn't help relieve my anxieties. As we passed in the hall, I asked, "Excuse me, can you tell me what is going on?"

Truthfully, I don't recall his answer, but the frightened look on his face, he may as well have said, "It's ok, everything's all right, but we are all going to die!"

The upper level was a mess. Every rack in the gifts shop was turned over onto the floor. Dishes in the restaurant were broken and scattered across the floor. Chairs were turned over. This is where I found my wife and two of our friends. We made our way to the upper deck, where we saw that water from the swimming pool had spilled out, washing chairs and tables over the ship's side and into the Gulf of Mexico. From the handrail I could see a long stream of floating debris, mostly pool furniture, and realized at that moment that people could have easily been washed overboard too. We felt a sense of urgency to find the other couple who traveled with us. It didn't take long and we were all accounted for. Relieved to know that we were all together, we then began to speculate as to what had happened. Why was the ship turned on its side?

The official explanation is that the ship's ballasts had become defective, but my theory is that the bump that we felt while having dinner on the first night was the ship hitting something, which caused a leak. The ship took on enough water that it affected the captain's ability to navigate the river, which is why we ran aground. The coast guard gave the go ahead for the ship to proceed once satisfied that the damage had been fixed. Once in the open Gulf, the ship began taking on water again. The ship's engineers calculated the amount and effects of the flooding and that is why the trip was shortened. Once the ship took on too much water, it listed to one side.

Regardless of the cause, upon our return to the Mississippi River, there they were in the sky above, helicopter news crews. We were on CNN twice in one trip.

Chapter 17: The English Teacher

Who Changed my Life's Direction

Ms. Bond must have dreaded the school bell which signaled the class I attended. We had a lot of class clowns in this tenth-grade English class, of which I was one. We were far more interested in finding humor in everything than we were in pronouns. We were very unfair and inconsiderate to Ms. Bond, and I'm not proud of that fact. She had every right to not like me. One day during the last week of the school year, just as the bell rang, she instructed me to stick around for a talk. I don't recall the conversation verbatim, but it went something like this…

"All of your test scores, homework, quizzes, and everything have been tallied, and your final grade is one point from passing. Everything has been considered except this one essay."

I don't remember what I said, but I remember how I felt. *Sick.* The thought of repeating the tenth grade….ugh.

"The content of your essay is good, but your grammar and punctuation, well that's a different story. This deserves a B plus, or an A minus. That little difference will make the difference between your passing and failing this class. Do you know that you can't go to the eleventh grade if you fail this class?"

I wasn't sure if she was taunting me before telling me I

would be in her class again next year or not. Was she torturing me before letting me know she was going get revenge for all the times I interrupted class by talking and laughing with my classmates?

"Is it important to you pass the tenth grade? Really important?" she asked.

"Yes, it is," I replied with a glimmer of hope.

"Why is it important to you?"

"Because, if I don't pass, I can't play football next year."

"Playing football is important to you?"

"Yes. Very important." I recall feeling a lump in my throat and knot in my stomach. Was she going to make me grovel? I would have.

"The grade that I assign to this essay is totally subjective. I can be generous and assign an A to this essay, giving a passing grade for this class, but first, I want to make a deal with you."

Here it comes, I thought.

"I will pass you under one condition. I determine who your English teacher will be next year. You must promise me that you won't ask to be transferred out of the class you are assigned. You will have to stick it out. Do you agree?"

She could have made me agree to anything at that moment, so of course I agreed.

With that behind me, I enjoyed the summer, hardly giving that frightening moment another thought. That was the only time I can close to failing in school.

When summer break was over and the new school year began, I went to my new classes, one by one. Nothing was out of the ordinary until I was seated in Ms. Sims' classroom. I looked around to see which of my friends were in this class. There were none. Not a single person in this classroom had ever been in any classroom with me in all the years of attending school. That was odd. So odd, it had never happened before.

There were some classmates who I recognized. The first one that I recognized was Brad Gordon, possibly the smartest kid in all of Pascagoula High School. He was a senior and I was a junior. Wait a minute, I thought. That guy over there is a brainiac senior too. He later became a brain surgeon. Everyone in the classroom was an overachiever who later became doctors, dentists, lawyers, and so on. Not only that, but they were also all seniors. I was the only junior in the class.

The bell rang and as my classmates exited the room, I

lingered a bit so no one would hear me tell Ms. Sims, "I think there is a mistake. I'm not supposed to be in this class."

"Why do you say that?" She asked.

"I'm a junior and everyone else in this class is a senior."

"This is the class your tenth-grade teacher assigned you, so she must have thought you were ready."

The conversation with Ms. Bond came back to me. This is her revenge! "Well, I hate to say it like this, but this class is full of smart kids. I don't belong in here."

Ms. Sims was a soft-spoken Southern lady. Not like Ms. Bond, who was very tough. In her soft voice, she said, "I understand you made a deal with Ms. Bond."

Oh crap – I realized they were in this together, and there is no way I'm going to pass the eleventh grade, I thought.

The next two weeks were what Ms. Sims called "reviewing sessions." She explained that this is when she would review everything, we were supposed to have learned last year, but after reviewing was completed, we weren't going to cover those topics again, because we were expected to know them. Knowing this was the Advanced English course, I knew that I had to pay closer attention. Plus, Ms. Sims presented the information in a fast-paced manner. There was no time for my mind to wander off subject. The kids in the classroom were there to learn. The one and only time I tried to crack a joke, no one laughed or encouraged me, but I got a couple of sneers from classmates.

The fast-paced method of teaching helped me to learn more in the first two weeks of that class than I had learned in the last two years of English classes. To my surprise, my final grade was a B plus! I never made less than an A in an English class again, even throughout college.

The following year, I entered and won first place in a statewide short story writing contest. That was the first time I realized I may have writing skills. If you've gotten this far in this book of short stories and essays, you might agree – I hope.

You might think that the title of this chapter is referring to Ms. Sims, but it's not. It was Ms. Bond who changed my direction. Either she saw potential in me – the good Lord only knows why or how – or she really wanted to exact revenge. I prefer to believe the former. Either way, her decision to pass me, with the conditions she established, change my opinion of myself.

This chapter is dedicated to Ms. Bond and Ms. Sims and all the other quality teachers who are truly dedicated to improving the lives of their students.

Chapter 18: The Romanian Rebel

During most of my life, the world was clearly divided between two competing ideologies, i.e., capitalism versus communism. The factions were often referred to as "East" and "West," with the East being communist countries that formed an alliance known as the "Communist Bloc," and the West calling itself the "Free World."

The principal of communism is that people exist to serve the state, but in those days, most people in the Western World believed that governments should exist to serve the people, which explains the self-description, "Free World."

Those in the East and West clearly knew who the enemies were; the communist Soviet Union and their proxies controlled half the world and the United States, and our allies controlled the other half. There was virtually no trade, travel, or communications allowed between the nations which were separated by an Iron Curtain (figuratively).

The center of power in the East was the Union of Soviet Socialist Republics (USSR, or the Soviet Union), which was an empire created by Russians. The Soviet Union's official policy was for their government to have total global control over all people and property. Their philosophy was that the end justified the means to achieve their goal. Nothing was more sacred than their utopian goal, in which everyone would be equal and unselfishly serving a higher cause – the state. Neither international law nor sovereign boundaries deterred them from their mission of world domination by the Communist Party. Numerous countries were invaded by the Soviet Union. Those who resisted were bombed by planes and tanks and brutalized by an unforgiving occupying force.

The only deterrent that the Communists respected was the United States' military and nuclear arsenal. The United States had drawn a line in the sand, so to speak, protecting its allies in western Europe and elsewhere. The Soviets knew that provoking a war with America could result in destruction of their nation.

The United States and its allies, the West, was keenly aware that war with the Soviets could also result in total annulation because the USSR likewise had enough nuclear weapons to destroy life on Earth. Both sides faced "mutually assured destruction" if either side started a nuclear war.

The rivalry between the competing factions was as fierce as any war could be absent of direct military conflict, so the conflict became known as "The Cold War." There were hot wars, called proxy wars between allies and third-world countries associated with the Cold War, such as the Korean Conflict and the Vietnam War, which could have easily led to a hot war, and potentially nuclear war between the East and West.

Everyone in the world knew of the possibility that someone on either side could trigger an event which could lead to worldwide nuclear holocaust, the end of life on Earth as we know it. There seemed to be no peaceful end to the conflict either. Looking at a world map, both the East and West controlled formidable territories with huge populations and enormous military and natural resources.

Most people accepted that the threat of instant evaporation was going to be a fact of life until it happened. A peaceful resolution was unfathomable, or in those days every American that I knew was willing to fight in the streets and kill or die for our country to prevent our families and decedents to be enslaved by a small elite class of communist rulers – and we believed that the citizens of the USSR were equally committed to forcing their way of life upon us.

The most significant landmark separating East from West was the Berlin Wall which was built by the communists to keep its citizens from fleeing to the West. Hundreds, maybe thousands, of Berliners were murdered by armed guards while trying to escape communism. This was our first clue that the citizens in the East were not as committed to communism as we were to democracy and freedom.

I watched in complete astonishment when the Berlin Wall was torn down in 1989 by the citizens of East and West Berlin. It was an extremely scary time for we had no idea how the USSR would respond. We wondered if this was going to be the catalyst for nuclear war. The USSR did not respond to the dismantling of the Berlin Wall, and as a result there were subsequent democratic revolutions that swept the Soviet Bloc countries. Each one had the potential of beginning World War III. Thankfully, the USSR did not respond, for unknown to us at the time, the West had won the war with its superior economy. The USSR was broke. Within a couple of years, the entire Soviet Union dissolved. The fall of the Berlin Wall was such an important event in the lives of every living person on this planet, then, now, and for the rest of human history, that I keep a piece of it in a case on my desk so that I can be thankful of the sacrifices of those who risked their lives resisting communism.

I've gotten to know people who lived on the other side of the Iron Curtain or other communist countries, some who risked their lives during that revolution.

Alisa Petukhov lives in Los Angeles selling Mercedes Benz for a living. Her father was a famous scientist for the Soviet Union. He has a rock on the moon named after him. Alisa said that despite her father's achievements, their apartment in Russia was the same as the custodian's apartment. There was no financial incentive in the Soviet Union to excel. The state provided a school dropout with the same home and salary as a notable scientist. The only exception being that members of the Communist Party received perks such as better jobs, higher salaries, and bigger and better homes, including vacation homes. In other words, there were millionaires and billionaires there, too, but there was no middle class.

I traveled to Nicaragua in 2008, where I had dinner in the home of Gorge Gonzales with him and his family. After dinner, we went for a walk. He explained that he owned the homes on both sides of the street, about ten in all. "When the Sandinista communists took over, men with guns showed up and claimed these homes for the communist party. They even tried to take the one that I live in, but I stood in the doorway with my gun, and they left." The people who took the homes in the name of the state were simply stealing the homes for themselves. They moved in and became non-rent paying squatters. The state condoned the activity until the Sandinistas were no longer in power. Gorge had to sue each squatter in court to have them removed. It took years, but by the year 2008, only two of his homes were still occupied by the communist squatters. "Can you guess which two are occupied by the squatters?" he asked.

It was easy to spot them. All but two of the homes and yards were well maintained. Their occupants had obvious pride in their homes. The two that were occupied by nonpaying squatters were a mess. Trash and tall weeds defined their yards. Windows were spray painted in some cases, and in others ransacked paper seemed taped in place of curtains.

The memory of that walk and talk with Gorge came to me when I was in Ecuador in 2015. I had just closed the huge gate that separated the upscale development rented to foreign tourists from the local village. None of the homes outside of the compound that I had just left had air conditioning or hot water. Most residents shared community showers.

There were openings in the concrete block exterior walls which served as windows, minus the glass. At night, I could see people lying asleep in their second-story bedrooms in some cases. The first home to my right was typical for the town. A man was sitting, his back to me, on a mound of dirt just feet away from his front door. I paused to notice that he was carefully placing ceramic tiles to enhance the border around his home's entrance. Despite being very poor by American standards, he had pride in the home that he had. Those who work to pay for their homes have pride of ownership, and those who don't, don't.

Backup a few years, to the year 1995 This is when I first met Corneliu Vaida. He was part of an exchange program between the United States and Romanian Chambers of Commerce to expose Romanians to capitalism. Through family connections, Corneliu ended up staying in my home and going to work with me for a week or so.

For all his life the state owned everything – every home and business were property of the state. Citizens were allowed to live in apartments owned by the state so long as they obeyed the state. They were given salaries in return for their labor, but the average salary for Romanians at that time was about US$100 per month.

Corneliu was overwhelmed by the wealth that he saw in Mississippi, the poorest state in the United States. Average people did not have cars in Romania, so the sight of teeming traffic and teenage drivers must have been amazing to him. Things that we take for granted such as fully stocked grocery shelves, heaping servings of food at restaurants, and the freedom to travel and speak our minds were all new experiences for him.

Corneliu described himself humbly as just an ordinary citizen. He did not seek fame, but like so many people throughout history, circumstances propelled him into a position to affect the lives of his countrymen for generations to come – if they can keep it, to borrow a line from Benjamin Franklin.

In the early months of 1989, no one could foresee the monumental changes coming. A person predicting the fall of the

Berlin Wall, or the collapse of the Soviet Union would not have been taken seriously. Romanians had no reason to believe that they would not always live under Soviet authoritarian rule, but the Berlin Wall was torn down, and millions of oppressed people living under communism were encouraged to rise up and demand freedom.

Corneliu was on his way to work when he encountered a group of protestors blocking his way. He tried to avoid becoming involved, so he detoured and took another route. It became more difficult to avoid the protestors with each passing day as the crowd size grew and grew, and so did the opposing military forces. The international press took notice and appeared on the scene. While trying to avoid the crowd, Corneliu found himself among a group of international reporters who began asking him questions in various languages. Fortunately for the world's press corps, Corneliu speaks at least five different languages. Soon he was being sought out by the press to give a local's perspective as to the happenings. As a result, he soon became the unintended spokesman for the rebellion. His picture was on magazine covers and in newspapers around the world. Fame is not always a good thing. Corneliu became a wanted man by the state which deemed citizens expendable. The following are Corneliu own words:

Because we are celebrating thirty years since the Romanian Revolution of December 1989 these days, considering the fact that the historical truth must be spread, acknowledged and, above all, respected, I will recount the things I lived and, particularly, felt those days ... and afterward.

The thirty years elapsed since the Revolution could not erase my memories of those times. The stories that you will hear in the following minutes belong to someone who, in those days, had the opportunity to be one of the most informed civilians involved in those events that took place in December 1989, in Timișoara.

As a result of an accidental set of circumstances, I was the only civilian who had access to the "Operations" office of the garrison headquarters Timișoara, after the days when Timișoara had been declared the first city free of communism. I was present at the broadcasts and manipulations in the office of the garrison commander, I could see the "battle log" ever since, but also the battle for power that took place among several groups of army and security. I attended the organizational naivety of the FDR (later FSN) Leading Committee in the Opera building. I became the first spokesman of the Army and the Revolutionaries to officially inform the foreign journalists who were beginning to assault Timișoara.

In the days when the riots emerged on the streets of Timișoara, I was a "young and restless" locksmith mechanic at the Motorcar Enterprise (formerly known as Tehnometal), and therefore, even from the first manifestations, I couldn't keep off them. It seems that I haven't healed yet...

My mother was a Reformed practitioner believer, a worshipper of the church where minister László Tőkés served. She would bring the minister food and firewood daily, so I was keeping track of what was happening both in the church and around it, even in the minister's family.

On the evening of December 16, my mother called and told me I should by no means come over – her place was 300 meters away from the Reformed Church – because "a big scandal was going on". Of course, I did not listen to my mother, and, on my way to St. Mary Square, I was run in by a militia van, where I joined a drunken citizen. I eluded apprehension, because a militiaman, who stopped the van in the Mărăști area, was my high-school colleague. He got me out of the van and that's all he told me: "Run home!"

But the next day I was back on the streets.

On Sunday, December 17, I wanted to take my three-year-old son to the Puppet Theater. I found out that the performance had been canceled.... Then, with the child in my arms, I tried to go to the Reformed Church to see what was happening. A line of secret police soldiers and civilians, most of them dressed in leather coats and jackets, were in the Küttl (Mocioni) Square, next to the belfry of the Orthodox church. I approached the line and they ordered me to stop, demanding that I left where I had come from. Because I was holding the baby in my arms, I obeyed the orders but… the unpredictable happened: my son suddenly shouted: "Down with Ceaușescu!". I broke into a run and saw, looking over my shoulder, how a civilian dressed in a leather jacket stopped two others who were set in pursuit of me. Later, in 1990, I would find out that the civilian's name was Gelu Popovici, he was a captain in the militia and became — until he was assassinated in 1999 — one of my best friends.

Toward noon, hearing that the events were getting hot at the county party headquarters, I contacted my friend Tiberiu Budău and we decided to go there as well.

Because we couldn't get into 23 August Blvd., as the road was blocked by army lines and armored vehicles, we decided to make a detour and go on Bega's bank, towards the small bridge that led into the Pioneers' Park.

Once there, we found a small group of protesters; however, they were standing, impressed by the military line and the four TABs (amphibious armored vehicles) that were stopped, engines running, on the street section that led to the "Decebal" Bridge.

Tibi and I wanted to cross the bridge, but we were stopped by a group of conscripted soldiers and an officer whose gun was out of its holster... "Stop! Back off! Don't try anything or we will start the fire!" the officer shouted.

We stopped and tried to convince him that we were paying a visit to a friend. The lie didn't work and the officer cocked his pistol. One of the soldiers, who was in front of him, slowly pulled out the loader of his AKM rifle to show us that they had no bullets....

However, fearing the officer, we backed off...

Once again arrived at the junction of Pestalozzi and Pârvan streets, we saw that quite a large group of protesters was coming toward us from the "Timişoreana" Beer Factory. When that group approached us and we united, two TABs took off from where they were stopped and started to chase us around the crossroads, aiming to break us apart.

One of the TABs followed the group of protesters I was part of and ran a woman down and killed her — two meters behind me — later, I found out that her name was Rozalia Popescu. I was faster and more fortunate, as I flung myself down the Bega embankment, down the small bridge that connected the crossroads with the Pioneers' Park. From there, I ran several tens of meters downstream, then I went up the street again and returned to the goddamn crossroads, asking the people at the windows and balconies across the street for empty bottles and gasoline, to set the armored vehicles alight.

Despite our desperate calls, no one in the crowd of people at the windows of the blocks across the street wanted to bring us empty bottles or to give us gas, except for a young man who brought us two raffia bags with empty beer bottles... so, along with my friend Tiberiu Budău, I attacked with empty bottles the TABs that were trying to scatter the group of protesters I was a member of, injuring an officer who had come out of a TAB's access hatch, right at his brow ridge.

On 20 December, after lunch, we went with the column of protesters, who were enthusiastic because the army had come to terms with us, to the county party headquarters. I had a spray with red paint, to detect cracks in metallic surfaces processed by cutting — graffiti sprays were not yet invented at that time — spray with which I had written anti-communist slogans on the wall of the Botanical Garden and block facades on Calea Torontalului, carefully guarded by my late friend, the lyric artist Marius Iuliu Mare.

There, in the crowd gathered in front of the county party headquarters, together with some colleagues from I.A.T, I was wondering "Nevertheless, where are the secret police agents?... they are swarming among us for sure!" As a result, we started to study the people around us attentively when — oops! — my gaze was drawn to a guy wearing a khaki sweatshirt, hooded… on the inside and with an oblique look. "How are you, buddy?" I said, friendly patting his back and I startled, feeling the shape of a… gun! "Catch him, he's armed!" — I shouted and my fellows, along with others around held him still. They almost lynched him, but we managed to hand him over to the ones inside, namely a militiaman and a revolutionary, who were guarding the entrance. We started to go around the building and, at a certain moment, I noticed that the guy held by us was escaping through the ground floor window, behind the county party headquarters, and ran toward the Bastion. We tried to reach him, but we failed…

The revolutionaries inside had not been out for a long time to communicate to us what they were negotiating with Dăscălescu.

The crowd was murmuring and started to scatter slightly. Some persons came and urged us to go to the Opera Square and to hold the Opera building, where, as some said, people had already entered. I felt that something had to be done, to give a boost to the crowd, to keep them on the spot, not to leave those who stood for us inside the building, because we risked leaving them to the militia and to the secret police forces that were for sure inside, as well.

I thought about spraying a slogan on the wall of the county headquarters. No sooner said than done! I got in front of the building wall, two people lifted me up, and for an instant I was scared, seizing how exposed I was. I knew I couldn't go back and decided to write something as... equidistant as possible, so I wrote: "People have won!"

Loud acclamations followed my move, people took the spray from my hand and, in about ten minutes, the entire frontispiece of the county headquarters was covered with slogans against Ceausescu and communism.

On the evening of December 22, I visited my mother, who was living on 6 March Blvd., and there I found a neighbor in the apartment. Gheorghe Toader, a retired secret police captain, who had taken refuge at my mother's place, afraid not to be killed, as there had been trials during that day, according to his own account. Watching "Revolution Live", the TVR (Romanian Television) broadcast, I noticed a person who was holding an object that looked like a control keypad and said the device was found in the basement of the TVR head office.

Seeing the keypad, the neighbor cried out with fear: "They will all blow up! TVR is a 'strategic objective' and can be blown up by typing a code on such a detonator!" He said he used to work on something like that in

Bucharest, in a special enterprise of Securitate (secret police). As I insisted, he finally agreed to write an anonymous statement, which I took personally to the garrison headquarters and I promised that I would not expose him.

Once I arrived at the garrison headquarters in the Piața Libertății (Freedom Square), I showed the letter to Colonel Mancu – who was by chance at the gate and who led me to Colonel Zeca – the garrison commander. Reading the statement brought by me, he called an army structure in Bucharest right away and he reported the content of the declaration. Afterward, he asked me to reveal the identity of the signatory, arguing that the one still holds vital information that would help to avoid new victims.

At first, I refused, but Colonel Mancu gave me his officer word that if Gheorghe Toader had proved to be in good faith, he would be safe.

Given the situation, I agreed to tell him the name and I had to drive with a patrol in an ARO off-road vehicle and pick the secret police officer from my mother's house. The outcome? Towards morning, I saw on the TV set in the commander's office how an officer came in front of the cameras and declared that the explosive that mined the Television building had been defused!

The next morning, in one of the walks to the garrison headquarters in Piața Libertății, I witnessed the arrival of a group of foreign journalists. Because foreign languages were not widely known in the army – besides Russian, someone needed to facilitate communication between journalists and army leaders. Knowing four languages, I came forward to be the translator.

Thus, a few hours later I was accepted as a spokesman by the commander. At the journalists' suggestion, we organized a press conference every evening, at the "Continental" Hotel's brasserie.

Because, on the morning of 23. December, I was shot upon on Brediceanu St. – from the roof of the IELIF building, I asked Colonel Zeca to hand me a weapon and to assign me to a group of military investigators, to detect and kill the shooters who made victims and decoy. These activities filled my nights, until New Year's Eve, when I finally got home to my wife. I mention that I wore the weapon only during night scour missions.

During the day, I was also the spokesman of the revolutionaries who were based in the Opera building, and their official news was sent by me to foreign journalists. I would go to the Opera building twice a day, to find out news or to send the correspondence between the garrison commander and the leaders of the Revolution.

The first press conference, attended by journalists and TV stations from all over the world, was held on the evening of 23 December, but the meeting was closed by journalists laid on their bellies because shootings were started outside against the "Continental" hotel. In the days that followed, until 31. December, I accompanied the representatives of the foreign press to the hot spots of the city, and, at night, we participated in actions of quarry and annihilation of the shooters together with the investigators directed by Major Bănescu.

I was part of the group of military and civilians who arrested Septimiu

Ta\şcău, the manager of GIGCL, on Christmas Eve. Guns were fired from his office window, at me as well, and the bullet fired by him passed through my hair!

As a result of the capture, a telescope gun was found on Ta\şcău and its barrel was still warm, with traces of soot and the specific smell of shooting.

I also saw an Arab citizen arrested; he was dressed in a black jumpsuit, like a tankman's, and as a response to my question "why do you shoot at us", he kicked me, even though his hands were tied. Both detainees disappeared from the garrison's arrest within 48 hours.

I narrate you all these only to tell you that the "myth of terrorists" was not a myth, but a reality, lived by many but known by few.

Rod Nordland, a "Newsweek" journalist, was among the important names of the international press arrived in Timişoara — he was the head of the Eastern Europe office. Another one was Ettore Mo, representing "Corriere della Sera."

Rod Nordland asked me to take him around the city, to various important targets. I also took him Traian Sima's house, the former Securitate leader of the Timiş county, as he managed to escape from home. Lots of stuff were stolen "officially" from his house, bags with money (lei and currency!), foreign food and drink, cigarettes and coffee, audio/video electronics were carried away…

Again together with Rod Nordland, I discovered the room in "Continental" where the secret police held the bugging/ translation equipment. I ran after the security guard who came to retrieve the devices, but he locked himself in another room. I broke the door, yet he was gone. He disappeared, though the room was on the fourth floor.

On 2 January, I left with Ettore Mo, from "Corrierre della Sera" for Mineu (Sălaj county), to make an interview with minister László Tőkés. We were among the first journalists to interview him. He was still guarded by the army.

March 1990, my office in the building of the county council. The phone rings.

- Hello, is this Corneliu Vaida?

- Yes. Who is this?

- Nevermind... Watch out, it's not OK that you listed as a witness for "The Timişoara Trial"!

- You don't say ... No shit?!

- I would be more cautious if I were you! Your son has just received an orange crate on your behalf... He might find one hard to chew!

I slammed the phone and made off from the County Council to the Iosefin neighborhood, in the house where my son was taken care of by his grandparents. I bustled in and saw the elders together with my son in the kitchen, as they were enjoying the crate with oranges on the table.

Without a word, I took the crate and sprang out the door, crossed the street and threw the crate into the Bega, under the astonished gaze of several passers-by and my family watching me dismayed from the gate.

- Why have you thrown my oranges away? Paul asked me, tears in his eyes...

- Don't worry, daddy will bring you other oranges tonight... And don't you ever accept anything from anybody, brought on my behalf! — I told the grandparents bluntly.

If you ask for my opinion nowadays, 30 years after the events of the Revolution, I can assert:

"There were two groups that fought against each other, the secret police and the army. Now we only know the winners… They are the crypto-communist gang of the 2. echelon.

I do not know what would have happened if the television headquarters had blown up on 22. December, what would have happened if the plan to slay the revolutionaries in the Opera building, which was stopped at the last moment, would have been completed, if the army in Timişoara had not fought back, action that emerged after Elena Ceauşescu had ordered that the city be wiped off the face of the earth!

The above-mentioned things are a synthetic, even hollow, description of those made and lived by me back in the days, as I wanted not to exceed two pages, which have actually become … four …

Feelings? Experiences? They were many and different: from the exaltation experienced at the news that "it started", the fear I felt in the militia van, the hatred, the perseverance and the helplessness facing the army that fired guns and killed people, the fear and, later, the enthusiastic carelessness as I was perched on the wall the county party council… the sadness that stroke me hearing the news that a friend was killed, the enthusiastic fervor and the unconscious courage that prompted me to leave, in order to scour houses' attics for terrorists who were shooting innocent civilians, the compassion for the wounded that I visited in hospitals together with the representatives of the international press and the pride to be part of the illusion of victory… all these culminating with the fear for the life of my child!

Yes, I mentioned the pride to be part of the illusion of that victory, a pride that turned into disappointment, frustration, and reproach over time. Yes, self-reproach, because I reproach myself for not finishing what I started back then!

Maybe someone else will do it nowadays… not compelled… younger or not, more prepared, more clearheaded, more thorough.

I must tell you that it wasn't easy for me to write these lines! Blurry memories and contradictory feelings overwhelmed me as I was writing. Nostalgia or anger, smile, and tears flew over my face while I was linking my ideas… However, there is one feeling that remains solid, the feeling of gratitude that, at that time, I did everything in my power to fight for the freedom of my people and the democratization of my country.

At the same time, I wrote these lines with sadness, with the sadness of someone who, although he owns an official acknowledgment of his deeds, signed by the president of the country, is — together with other fighters for the victory of the Revolution — disregarded by the state and by most of his fellow citizens.

Nowadays, the word "revolutionary" has gotten a pejorative meaning... Anyway, I was, I am and I will be a fighter for my freedom and the freedom of my fellow citizens! With or without written proof.

Corneliu's concerns about today's perception of socialism and the revolutionaries who fought against them are not unfounded. It's been said that if you do not know your history, you are destined to repeat it. According to press reports, 30 percent of all young Americans polled in 2019 stated that they favored socialism. They are too young to know what it meant live under the threat of nuclear holocaust or possible communist invasion and subjugation.

Corneliu being interviewed in 1989

(Wearing the beret in the picture above)

Corneliu N. Vaida (right) in 2022

Acknowledgment

Special thanks to Norman Ruble, Corneliu Vaida,

Anna Breland, and my mother, in heaven

Coming Soon:

Me and You and Kalamazoo

The Adventures of Kalamazoo

A children's book series

Visit My Website and Select the

"My Books" Page

www.Breland.biz

to order your copy.

Support starving artists:

Please be kind and review this book.

www.ingramcontent.com/pod-product-compliance
Lightning Source LLC
Chambersburg PA
CBHW070455300726
48975CB00007B/2177